For the Love of a Grand

For the Love of a Grand

Elizabeth Russell
and
Rev. Allan H. Charles

VANTAGE PRESS
New York

Cover design by Susan Thomas

FIRST EDITION

All rights reserved, including the right of
reproduction in whole or in part in any form.

Copyright © 2008 by Elizabeth Russell and
Rev. Allan H. Charles

Published by Vantage Press, Inc.
419 Park Ave. South, New York, NY 10016

Manufactured in the United States of America
ISBN: 978-0-533-15928-4

Library of Congress Catalog Card No.: 2007908150

0 9 8 7 6 5 4 3 2 1

To Theodore and Asia Roberts

Contents

Acknowledgments ix
Introduction xi

One	When Love Bears All	1
Two	When Love Endures All	21
Three	When Love Conquers All	41
Four	When Love and Hope Interact	58
Five	When Love Believes and Provides	80
Six	When Love Abides	99

Acknowledgments

I wish to thank:

My husband, who loves this child as though she were his own, for his patience, tolerance, and kindness toward her.

My sister, Berta, for giving not only of her time but also for providing many hours toward the child's care and enjoyment.

My friend, Laura Trayvick, who tutored her and assisted in her early education by supplying so much that she had lost in being kept out of school.

My pastor, Carlton Flanigan (now deceased), who encouraged me to rescue this child and for the advice, which was needed very much, during my periods of frustration.

Yolanda Byrd, one of Eara's closest friends, who shared moments of joy in her youthful and young adult years.

Nikki Wilt, a close friend of Eara, who was a beacon of encouragement and hope during her moments of despair and despondency.

Introduction

This is a story about a beautiful little girl born to intelligent, well-reared parents, neither of whom was apparently ready for parenting. The child, born in the Bronx, New York, suffered abandonment, hunger, neglect, poverty and finally renal failure, after being moved from pillar to post.

More importantly, the content and various contexts of this story presents the very active role of the grandmother who provided the necessary nurturing required for the adequate development and growth of her granddaughter. She was a grandmother who personified and epitomized "LOVE" in action. She was not only a positive role model but also a grandmother who exemplified the essence of "Agape Love" that Paul, the Apostle, exhorts in 1 Corinthians 13:1–13.

Love in action was exemplified in the following way: in order to provide the child a comfortable, stable home and the necessary things for properly rearing a child, the child's grandparents were able to clothe her and take her into a loving home, provide a clean and comfortable environment and take proper care of her. There existed a loving relationship between the child an the grandparents. However, after three years, the mother intervened and the child wanted to be with her mother.

Although many grandparents have found it difficult in trying to rear their grandchildren (due to parental behavior, suffering through double and triple jeopardy from adversaries within and without, environment and cultural effects, and dealing with the child's peer pressure(s), et al.), this little girl's grandparents found that:

- It can be—and was—a rewarding experience during their retirement years.
- The children can benefit from the care and attention given to them in their critical, formative, and young adult years in life.
- The bond between grandparents and grandchildren should never be broken.
- In many cases and/or situations what the grandparents considered as assistance often resulted in parents' resentment and sometimes jealousy rather than gratitude.
- Most of all, it has proven that prayer and constant contact with God is the answer to the problems in everyone's life, both young and adult alike.

Finally, this story attempts to inform its readers that (in spite of the many obstacles and the bad outweighing the good experiences) this little girl has been able to survive and has grown into a beautiful young woman, via the constant overseeing and loving dedication of her grandparents. In particular, it is through the unceasing, unwavering, stop at nothing and no matter what the cost, love shown by the grandmother, that this little girl became a woman that not only loves God but one who also cherishes God's blessings in life and one that God can use to inspire other young and old women and men in life to hold on—no matter what they are going through.

For the Love of a Grand

One
When Love Bears All

When LOVE beareth all things LOVE has the power to conquer the fear of the inevitable and the unforeseen. LOVE has the power to: protect, redeem, rescue, shield, take on unwarranted responsibility, under-gird, uphold and uplift. LOVE has the power to: bring salvation, resolution and wholeness from all of life's unpleasant, un-seedy, and unwarranted circumstances that have an effect upon one's well-being and welfare.

Frances (Fran) Baldwin was a proud woman of short stature, about 5'2" tall. Nonetheless she stood tall from chest up to the top of her head. Fran was a very amiable, intelligent and intellectual type of person. She was a determined person, with a quick mind, who took ownership of whatever task she endeavored to resolve. She was a person who always greeted everyone with a welcoming smile. She frequently, lovingly and passionately beared all, did all and gave her all for all.

Moreover, Fran exemplified this forebearing type of Love through the growing up years of her precious granddaughter Eara Baldwin. Frances' reward for such endearing endeavors allowed her to become the custodial guardian of her granddaughter by the Civil Court action herein described.

"Mr. Baldwin, your mother may be proud of you, but

you should be proud of your mother for what she is doing." These words, stated by the Court Referee, concluded the action granting temporary custody of Eara, Todd Baldwin's eight-year-old daughter, to his mother, Frances Baldwin, sixty-five years of age, an arthritic having had recent hip replacement surgery, and who had retired five years earlier. Yet to her surprise and wonderment, the grandmother was filled with anxiety! Why? Yes she was happy because of her love for the child, but also she was fearful, lest she may not be able to adequately fulfill the responsibilities being placed upon her.

Who else, indeed, was there to save and rescue this beautiful little girl from the emotional "roller coaster" life, which had been hers from the time she was born? Like so many other grandparents Fran (Frances) had come to the rescue. Thus began another phase in the child's life. But let us look in retrospect at what that all-bearing type of love brought this child through before and after she was eight.

Eara was born October 17, 1973 in New York, New York. When learning of the mother's (Andrea's) pregnancy, the grandparents were ecstatic. Todd, the father, was thirty-nine years old at the time, and his parents had given very little thought to ever having a grandchild.

Todd was a robust man who wore a heavy mustache. He considered himself a "dresser." He was about 5'10" tall and about 210 pounds. He was a man who portrayed a bully like Sampson. He not only loved women and strong drinks but also loved "weed derivatives." Yet, on the sober side of life, Todd was a "budding" actor, having played roles in a number of famous Broadway shows, several television series, videos and at least five movies. In addition, he had served in the U.S. Air Force and later became interested in drama. His whole life was encapsulated, encompassed, laden, and overcoated with drama.

The mother, Andrea Hall, at age twenty-nine, ten years Todd's junior, was a college dropout. A woman with years of cross-breeding in her blood as indicated by her smooth mulatto complexion. She had dark brown perceiving eyes. She was about 5'8" tall and thin like a bean post, with big breasts. She possessed street-wise smarts and survival skills. One who became strongly addicted to smoking cigarettes and drugs.

At the first meeting of the two women, as in many strange cases and unfamiliar and unknown circumstances, there seemed to be a bit of evasiveness between the mother and the mother-in-law.

When Eara was two months old, Fran, upon hearing of a tour going to New York, decided to go and see her new grandchild. Todd did not inform Andrea that she was coming. In any event, upon arrival, Todd met the tour bus at the hotel and took his mother to the apartment where they were living in the Bronx.

Fran found the apartment very bleak and somewhat uncomfortable. There was very little food in the refrigerator. Fran nevertheless decided to spend, at least, the one night with them in order to become acquainted with her new grandchild.

So excited, she could hardly sleep. Early the next morning, Fran decided to arise from an emotional, sleepless night and go into the room where Eara was also awake. She dried Eara and changed her diaper and put her into bed with her. Around 7 A.M., Fran decided to arise, took Eara in her arms and went into the room where Todd and Andrea supposedly were asleep. They were awake and told her to enter. To her great surprise, both of them were lying there smoking marijuana. While

Fran had suspected Todd of the habit, she was greatly shocked to see his wife indulging. What thoughts immediately went through her mind on getting acquainted with this daughter-in-law to be? Only Heaven knows the answer to this question. Not being one to hold her tongue and peace, she immediately started lecturing them!

"Have you two lost what little sense you have left in what you call as a brain in your heads? No self-conscious and respectable parent, in his or her right mind, would or should be smoking such addictive, dangerous, debilitating, and harmful junk anywhere near his or her infant child, especially a child that is already full of congestion."

Immediately, an argument ensued. Todd was the first to lash out, followed by Andrea.

"Smoking pot is no worse than smoking cigarettes!"

"If Eara is addicted to marijuana, it did not just happen. I've been smoking this and other crack stuff since my early days in high school and college, which were long before I met your son. It's imbedded in my system. In fact, I was the one who turned him on to this marijuana and how to get treatment to come out of this addiction, should he choose to do so."

Upon this type of rebuttal from her son and Andrea, Fran decided arguing with fools is a waste of time and so she thought to herself it is better that I just forget the whole discussion. It was devastating to think that her grandchild's parents were doing drugs.

After lying around and getting high all morning until about noon, Todd announced that he had a rehearsal that afternoon and he left around that time. However, before he left, Fran had given Todd some money and asked him, "Please, buy some food and milk for the baby." Fran must have had a senile lapse. Why would she do such a thing, instead of asking questions and undertaking this chore herself? No one gives someone doing drugs "free money."

After Todd was gone, Fran and Andrea had a short conversation about their marriage. Andrea had very little to report concerning this sensitive subject.

She did say, "Todd gives me very little money, and whenever he does, he always comes back and takes it back from me. Like I am not trustworthy or something!"

The only thought that crossed Fran's mind was "Well . . ." They changed subjects and Fran lovingly focused on Eara's needs.

Later that afternoon, Andrea and her sister, Lee, went shopping. Lee was tall like Andrea. Her looks resembled her younger sister very much. She was a pleasingly plump person with a jovial smile. Like Fran she cared very much about her fellow human beings and was always very compassionate about others and their problems.

While Andrea and Lee were out shopping, this made Fran happy because now she felt she would have the entire afternoon to lovingly spend with Eara. In the meantime, other plans were to go to the theatre for the evening performance of the Broadway show in which Todd was then appearing. However, approximately three to four hours later, Andrea and her sister, Lee, came in. Andrea did not have time to introduce her sister but immediately went into the bathroom and threw up upon the window. Lee and Fran introduced themselves. Again, the awful odor of marijuana filled the whole room and apartment. It was this condition that made Fran decide not to spend another night in that apartment, but to go to the hotel where the tour group was staying.

After getting dressed for the evening plans, all left in a cab. They dropped Lee and Eara of at Lee's home and

Andrea and Fran went to the theatre. After the performance, Todd, Andrea and Fran had a late dinner. Todd and Andrea walked Fran to the hotel, which was within a few blocks from Broadway and where Fran had decided to spend the night.

Eara was eight months old the next time Fran saw her. During this time frame, The Masonic Order of The Imperial Shriners' Club was honoring Fran's husband, Jess, with a banquet. Jess was a big strapping Shriner, 6'4" tall, about 250 pounds. He was a man who possessed enormous strength. He had huge hands that could choke the life out of anything. Yet he was a caring man, who always wore a gentle smile on his face. He also looked at the good in everyone rather than to focus on other's negative side.

Naturally, the honoree's family attended these affairs, and Jess wanted Todd and his family to be there. Jess wanted Todd and his family to come home and be with him and his mother and family and friends in Dayton, Ohio. For this occasion Fran rented a bed, playpen and a high chair so that Eara could be comfortable in her new surroundings and environment. Out of deep, spiritual love for this child, Fran left no stone unturned. She bought baby food, diapers, and everything else that the baby would need. The afternoon on which Todd and his family arrived, Fran took Andrea and Eara to a shopping center and purchased all new clothes for the baby. Fran thought the clothes the parents brought with them, for the child, were hardly presentable.

In addition to wanting Todd and his family present for The Masonic Order of the Imperial Shriners' Club banquet honor, Fran had entertained and planned other thoughts in mind. With the parents' permission, Fran made arrangements to have Eara christened in the grandparents' church on Sunday.

Rev. Carlton Flanigan, the local Pastor, conducted the major parts of the Ritual or Service of Baptism. (Which is the Ritual or the Sacrament of Baptism by the reading of: the Scriptures, the Words of Exhortation, the responsibilities of parties involved with the life of the individual child or adult, and, the naming of the child or adult being welcomed into the Household of God, and the sprinkling of water on the child's and/or adult's forehead three times in the name of The Father, The Son and The Holy Ghost.) Jess' brother, who was a minister, did the actual christening, the latter part of the ritual.

All during the Church Service, Jess held Eara and she was perfectly contented, lying and/or sitting up in his lap and occasionally turning herself away from his gentle, smiling face. She was a beautiful baby and one who seldom cried.

The "Christening Dinner" was held at the grandparents' home, in the afternoon immediately following the 11 A.M. Morning Worship Service, and all went well until the evening. Why? Well, shortly after finishing his meal, Todd left the gathering to go out with some of his carousing, drug-imbibing friends and he did not return until about 5 or 6 P.M. Fran was not pleased with this scene. Fran met him at the back door to the kitchen, as he was trying to sneak back into the house. She immediately let him have a few choice words or so.

"Boy, for once, you could and should have stayed with your family and away from those good for nothing, drug-addicted, so-called friends of yours. Look at you. You are a disgrace! This was a very important day of celebration for your daughter and family and friends who have been positive role models in your life. Why did you have to go and mess it up?"

Todd responded, "Woman, you need to mind your own holier than thou business! I am a man and I can do as I please and I can take care of my family without any unprofessional help from you and your phony family and friends. This whole day has been nothing but a show!"

This confrontation nearly turned the whole day into a fiasco, as they went on for fussing at each other for 5–15 minutes longer. Fran decided forgiveness for the fool is the best way to end this mess and to lovingly get back to her granddaughter and those who were still present after the dinner.

As if the earlier events in the evening were not enough to upset Fran, well, Todd and Andrea had another surprise in store for her. At the time Andrea and Todd came, nothing had been said about the length of their visit. Nonetheless, Andrea decided that she would spend a few days and Todd and Eara would stay for a longer period of time. It was during the following conversation, that the first inkling of Andrea's wanting the grandmother to keep the child was revealed.

Immediately, Fran responded, "I am still working every day and my belief and conviction is that every baby should have the opportunity and time to bond with its mother before being separated from her."

Andrea did not like this response and turned to Todd and said, "Let us turn in for the night." For the next three days, not a whole lot of conversation transpired between the parents and the grandparents, except for good morning, good afternoon or good night and enjoy the day. Andrea left after about three days and Todd and Eara stayed until the following weekend. When the time came for Fran to say her goodbyes, Fran's heart was very heavy, so much so, that she began to cry as she left them at the airport. During the parting moments, Fran felt then that trouble lay ahead and she wondered if Andrea really wanted this child!

Shortly after the Dayton, Ohio visit and after returning to New York, Andrea left Todd in New York City to go to Troy, New York. Andrea told Todd that she planned to finish her education. However, her main reason for moving to Troy was that she went there to live with her father and grandmother (Jethro Thomas Hall and Marilyn Mosianna Hall).

Her grandmother (affectionately known as grandma Moses Hall) was the housekeeper for her father. Grandma Moses liked to chew "snuff." She was a powerful woman about 5'2" tall. She was a wonderful lady of light complexion. Ancestral ties indicated she was a cross between Cherokee, Comanche and Afro-American. She did not hesitate to demonstrate her quick wit and rebuttal skills when in the midst of an adversarial conversation, especially in the defense of the downtrodden.

Andrea's father and mother had separated. Her mother returned to Texas from where the family had originally come. Jethro was a 6'1" tall man, about 160 pounds, with a very dark complexion from working as a laborer in the Texas heat from sun up to sundown for days on end. He was now an aged man with wrinkled skin and toothless. Every other word out of his mouth was a curse word, especially when he had difficulty trying to roll his own cigarettes.

Many of Andrea's traits were derived from her father. However, the underlying story behind all of Andrea's façade of moving to Troy with her grandmother and Jethro was that it later turned out to be an actual separation between she and Todd. They never lived together again after that time. Even though there were many subsequent visits to the grandparents in Dayton, Ohio, there was clear evidence of no husband and wife togetherness. This certainly put Eara's life in a continuum of turmoil.

So Fran being the ever concerned and loving grandmother, she often called and stayed in close touch with Eara. From time to time, Fran also sent money to help with support, as she was certain Todd gave little or no support of his child. It was to Fran's benefit to be able to call because so often while living in New York City, Todd and Andrea's telephone would be disconnected and she was unable to stay informed as to the child's welfare. By calling Andrea's father, Jethro, when Fran could not reach Todd or Andrea, he was very cooperative in giving information regarding Eara.

As time passed, Eara was now almost two years old and in the fall of 1975 Fran became very lonely to see Eara. Hence, she contacted a cousin, Larry Byrd, who lived in a nearby city (approximately 125 miles east of Dayton, Ohio), and asked him to help her drive to New York. Jess was working and could not get off from work at the time. The plans were to arrive in Troy on Friday evening, October 27, 1975 and to leave on the following Monday October 30, 1975 around 10 A.M. So Fran called Andrea to make hotel arrangements for cousin Larry and her. Instead, Andrea invited them to stay in her apartment.

Upon arrival, no one was there. After waiting for at least an hour, Fran and cousin Larry went to a public phone and Fran called Andrea's father's home. The grandmother, Moses, told Fran that Jethro was in Texas at the time. The grandmother also stated that she had no idea where Andrea and the baby were. After waiting for at least another hour, Fran and Larry decided to drive off and they stopped by a neighborhood grocery store. To their surprise, shortly thereafter, Andrea, with Eara, drove up and stopped at the same neighborhood grocery store.

Immediately Fran went on her usual tirade:

"Where have you been with my precious baby? What is going on here?"

Andrea did not respond to Fran's questions, but instead she walked away mumbling to herself and then asked them to follow her to the apartment. When they arrived at the apartment, Andrea showed Fran the room where she was to sleep. In the room there was only a mattress and a set of springs on the floor, no bedstead at all. Andrea and Eara slept on cots in another room. Cousin Larry was left to fan for himself.

Slick, fleet-foot, 155-pound, street-smart, cousin Larry was accustomed to being left out. After years of experience of being mistreated and groveling, he had no problems concerning being able to fan for oneself. He had confidence that his good looks, his wave-like hair style, his smooth and slick tongue and his eloquent dress manner would allow him to overcome any situation attempting to prevent him from providing for himself. He had all evening and the night to fulfill his task.

Nonetheless, the next morning, Andrea left saying that she was going to the library to study. Before leaving, Andrea, told Eara to take a bath and wash her hair. Eara was nearly two years old. Not knowing any better, the child was washing her hair in her bath water. This irritated Fran a whole lot. So Fran gave her a proper bath and then washed her hair, as it should have been done.

There was very little food in the refrigerator, but finding some Bisquick and lentils, Fran made pancakes for Eara and herself and they ate breakfast. This was surviving at all costs. Andrea, expecting them to be hungry and starving, was instead surprised when she returned home a short time later and found them lovingly happy and joyful, under the circumstances.

On Saturday evening, they drove to Albany, New York, to a shopping mall where Fran bought a pair of shoes for Eara. After walking around for a while, Andrea bought a half-gallon of Boone's Farm Wine. Lying as usual, she told them, "In case you are wondering about this wine purchase, I bought this for a picnic on Sunday." The only response Fran could muster up was a frown on her face.

Immediately after returning to the apartment, Andrea went upstairs with her bottle of wine and said, "I am tired and I am going to lie down for a little while." Instead she changed her clothing and went out without saying a word, around 5 P.M. However, a few hours later, while Fran, Larry, Eara and another friend, Myrtle Beach (whom Fran met on an earlier visit to New York), were out consuming a cheap evening meal, Fran sparingly turned her head to look out the window where they were sitting. She noticed Andrea openly carousing up to a white man while in his car, parked in a space next to the building. The only response Fran could utter was, "My, My, My. Where, how and why did my son meet such a woman? What type of mother can spawn and neglect such a beautiful child as this for drugs and prostitution?" The rest of the company at the table became curious and looking out the same window wondered the same sentiments.

Having returned to the apartment and after putting Eara and herself to bed, Fran awakened several times during the rest of Saturday night and during the wee hours of Sunday morning. Being in this strange apartment, Fran also got up and peeped into Andrea's bedroom to see if Andrea was there. But Andrea had not come home yet. By 6 A.M. Sunday morning, very upset, Fran called Andrea's grandmother to ask if she had seen Andrea. Fran was told that perhaps Andrea had stayed all night with a friend. Fran then bathed and dressed Eara, packed her bags and a bag of clothes for Eara. She then made a reservation to spend the night at the hotel where cousin Larry was staying. Cousin Larry came and picked up Fran and Eara and took them to the hotel. Late Sunday afternoon Fran, Larry, Myrtle and Eara went to Andrea's grandmother's home for dinner.

When Andrea finally came home to her apartment around 5 P.M., Sunday evening, she offered no apologies, had no comments as to why or where she had been or anything about having stayed away for twenty-four hours. Fran, sensing that something was amiss, asked if she could take Eara home, to Ohio, with her on Monday. Andrea gave her permission. Fran, Larry and baby Eara left as soon as they could get all packed on Monday morning to get out of New York.

On the return trip from New York, Fran dropped cousin Larry off at his home in Lancaster, Ohio and continued on to Dayton, Ohio. Meanwhile Eara slept (like a good baby) with her head in her grandmother's lap (no seat belts or baby-car seats at that time). Thank God the safety regulations were not in effect at that time. Fran would have gotten a ticket for sure.

Jess was overjoyed to see them upon their arrival. Eara was able to spend Christmas of 1975, as well as the rest of December 1975 and all of January of 1976 with them. Fran and Jess learned to love her and enjoyed her so much. Fran found it a pleasure to dress-up Eara in pretty little dresses and ribbons. Eara truly resembled a beautiful, little, talking and walking doll. The grandparents had very little to no problems with Eara and she seemed to be very happy and almost never cried. What a blessing! Fran even potty-trained her while she had this opportunity to do so.

During this time Eara and her "grampa" (as she called him) became great buddies. Every place he went she wanted to go with him. Finding a baby sitter was no problem because everyone who came to know Eara loved her and she was such a contented and good child. She was happy wherever they took her.

Toward the end of January 1976, Andrea called and said she was coming for Eara. Although the grandparents realized she had to leave, they became very sad. For hours after they boarded the plane for New York, Fran and Jess drove around, with lumps in their throats, crying. It was difficult for them to go home, knowing that Eara would no longer be in their immediate presence. Each night Fran prayed to God, asking God, "Please protect this child and God guide Andrea as to how to properly rear and train up this child, in the way she should go, so that she'll never depart from it as she grows older."

In the summer of 1976 Andrea called again and said that she, her sister Lee and her father were driving to Houston, Texas and would stop in Ohio on the way. She added if Fran wished, Eara could visit with her and they would pick her up on the return trip to New York. This, of course, made Fran and Jess very happy for at least the four weeks or so during that summer Eara was with them. This visit also allowed the grandparents to meet Eara's other grandparent (Andrea's father, Jethro) for the first time. More importantly, Fran and Jess were becoming more and more attached to Eara each time she visited. Each time she left it was becoming harder for them to accept her leaving. Out of loving this child so much, crying became inevitable.

During the Thanksgiving week of 1976, Todd and Andrea met again, for the first time in a long time, in Dayton, Ohio. Todd had been working in California at the time. Andrea and Eara traveled by car from New York to Dayton. The car was very old. Its tires were worn to within 1/32" of tread. When Andrea informed Fran and Jess that she was also intending to drive to Texas from Dayton in that same car with the same bad tire conditions, Fran could hardly stand the thoughts of it. Heaven forbid if the car broke down, if the tires became punctured, if an accident occurred!!! Nonetheless, it was snowing very hard the day Andrea and Eara left. There was nothing that Fran and/or Todd could say to change Andrea's mind. Fran lost it, became very upset and livid. Todd gave up in disgust, after rationalizing for years Andrea does what Andrea determines she is going to do. This, and other hints along the way, made Fran realize it was very obvious that Andrea and Todd were not living as man and wife.

To rescue Eara from such dysfunctional and separated parents, in June of 1977, Fran and Jess drove to New York to get Eara. While in New York, they also visited Andrea's grandmother, Moses, who was by then in a nursing home after having suffered a stroke. The next morning after making the visitation, they gathered Eara and her things and left for the return trip home to Dayton.

By now Eara was old enough to be enrolled in Vacation Bible School, being held at Wayman Chapel A.M.E. Church. A part of each day during the remainder of Eara's summer visit, she was also enrolled in nursery school at another nearby church. This opportunity allowed Eara to have the experience of learning new things and playing with other children. Eara enjoyed and bonded well with the other children and she enjoyed the field trips the nursery school supervisors took them on.

Above and beyond Vacation Bible School and nursery school activities, many times during this summer session, Fran would take Eara to the park where they had a swimming pool. From this experience, Eara was able to learn to swim very well. Fran was quite proud of the certificate, which Eara won at the end of the summer as an A-1 swimmer.

Fran being Fran, she was also a woman who feared, loved, and worshiped God, and, therefore, she stopped at nothing to see to it that her precious little granddaughter was being trained up in the way she should go.

So during this summer of 1977, Eara also got to learn and enjoy attending and learning "Bible Stuff" in Sunday school and church each and every Sunday morning. She also got to enjoy riding on the church bus, which would pick her up and take her to church, when her grandparents temporarily became unable to do so.

But one Sunday morning while sitting in church, Fran noticed tears streaming down Eara's cheeks. Upon asking what was wrong, Eara responded, "Grams, I love you and I love Mommy too and I don't know whether to stay or to go home." Fran understood Eara's apprehension. There were so many opportunities lovingly given her while she was with her grandparents that were not available at home with Andrea, yet Eara loved and missed her mother. By this time, Fran really wanted her to stay with them, but with "Agape Love," Fran wanted Eara to be certain as to where she wanted to stay. Eara decided she wanted to go home. This decision pierced deep and cut Fran to the bone, but with compassionate love Fran understood.

In the fall of 1977 Eara was now four years old, old enough to talk a great deal. Sometime shortly after her birthday (October 17, 1977), Eara decided she wanted to visit Gramma Fran and Grampa Jess again. It was during this visit that much information came out about her home life. Not being one to pry things out of a child, Fran tried, but just could not disregard some of the things, which Eara said. Eara spoke quite often and seemed quite fond of a fellow named Robby Porter. It was finally concluded that Robby and Andrea were living together. She told that at night while Mommy was working, Robby was her baby sitter and often took her to see a movie for entertainment. Although a bit amusing, one morning when she had a stomachache and asked Fran to rub some "halcohol" on her tummy, Eara further revealed that this was what Robby did to Mommy when she had a tummy ache. Eara also spoke of the night when she, Mommy and Robby were in bed. These and other revelations terribly upset Fran. So Fran became livid again and decided to call and threatened to do something about it if Andrea didn't discontinue some of Robby's and her behavior.

"What is this godless behavior you are condoning and letting a fellow named Robby perform with and before the innocent eyes of my granddaughter? Do I need to call the Child's Services Bureau in your city to have Eara removed from your custody forever?"

Andrea became profoundly annoyed and replied, "Call whom you wish. You'll never win this case! Now listen up, you holier than thou, busybody, Robby is a neighbor and one of the few good friends of mine, who I can count on. He has my back and I cover for him. Plus, he is very fond of and protects all the kids in the neighborhood. There is no hanky panky going on between the two of us. We help each other out to make ends meet for the good of the whole. That's all!"

On the latter response, Fran was afraid Andrea would not allow Eara to come visit her Ohio grandparents again. However, to show that she can let bygones be bygones, Andrea did say she would let Eara come and visit her Ohio grandparents again and not punish Eara for running off with the mouth. After several weeks, Andrea and a friend came for Eara. They stayed the weekend and a Sunday night, both of them went out and upon their return, it appeared both of them were under the influence of drugs and alcohol. Actually this was the first time Fran had ever seen Eara cry while leaving with her mother.

As time passed, once again, in May of 1978, Andrea called and said that she was going to Houston, Texas for a vacation and would drop Eara off in Ohio to visit and pick her up on the way back to New York. This trip, it turned out, had become more than just for a vacation. Apparently, Andrea had some other prospective plans in mind.

Later that summer of 1978, Jess bowled in a tournament in Detroit, Michigan. A suite was reserved in a nearby Howard Johnson's Motel. Jess took Fran and Eara to the bowling tournament. Eara thoroughly enjoyed playing games in the bowling alley. At the bowling alley, she met two little friends whose grandparents also brought them to the tournament. The three of them had a great time together.

After returning to Dayton, later that summer the three of them were back in Detroit, Michigan. Jess' family met in Detroit for a family reunion. During this event, Fran discovered that Eara loved being the center of attention and seemed to have a way of attracting the other youngsters. It was obvious that her personality was becoming one, which was not easily ignored. She was eager to be surrounded by friends, sharing with them and inviting them to visit with her. She liked being with others rather than being alone. Noting these developments made Fran very happy. Fran became very happy because she felt that all of this was indicative of the fact that Eara was adjusting to the environment, in which she was living. Fran became very happy because it appeared that Eara was no longer staying more to herself.

It was, as always, a very enjoyable summer and it seemed as if the time passed so quickly.

As the summer was coming to a close and fall was approaching, a season of new endeavors was on the way for Eara. The opening day of the school year grew close and not having heard from Andrea, Fran was concerned that Eara may not get to enter pre-kindergarten school for her first year, even though she would not be five years old until October 17, 1978. With September fast approaching, in order to attempt to get the child to Houston in time to start pre-school, Fran and Jess sent her by plane to her mother. However, Fran later learned that during this first year, Andrea kept Eara out of school for little or no reason at all. As a matter of fact, Fran learned that Eara's first year was briefly started in Houston, but finished in Troy, New York.

So, from infancy to the time Eara reached five years old, Eara's grandmother Fran—by, through and with FOREBEARING LOVE—not only went above and beyond the call of duty—to show compassion and forgiveness to those adults in her life who could lead Eara astray—but also went above and beyond the call of duty—to show she had become the source that:

- Kept the child from becoming a dope addict like her parents.
- Provided clothing, food, the fundamental joys of life, a shelter in the time of a storm.
- Became her sturdy bridge over troubled waters.
- Provided the security a child needs to trample over life's rickety bridges when parents fail to fulfill their custodial responsibilities.
- Exemplified the compassion and strength a child needs to leap over life's walls of misery.
- Provided comfort at the midnight hour, early in the morning, and at noon day hour.
- Provided the comfort and confidence that would: wipe the tears away, sit up with you when lonely or left alone, bring blessings beyond belief, mend the scars and heal the wound, go through hoops of fire and leap over walls to rescue and save the innocent.

Two
When Love Endures All

When LOVE endureth all things: LOVE can withstand false accusations, lack of compassion, deceit. LOVE can withstand gripes, harm, hate, and hurt. LOVE can withstand intense jealousy, lying lips, nothingness, pain and personal prejudices. LOVE can withstand sounding brass, suffering, struggling through battles, threats and tinkling cymbals.

To find LOVE like this, let us look at what Fran and Jess must go through to move Eara through life's seasons of good times and seasons of turmoil from five years old to her early formative years in elementary school and society.

During the summer of 1979, after Eara's first year in school, Fran learned that Andrea took Eara to Todd in New York City and that Andrea told Todd he could have Eara and she left Eara there with him.

Simultaneously, Fran learned that Todd was going with a woman, who at the time had a daughter Eara's age. The good that came out of this relationship was that both of the children attended their second year of school at the same school and Eara seemed to be doing well. Yet Fran was very much concerned at the hidden agendas. Why? Fran was well aware that Todd was an entertainer, an actor and a "man of the streets." Fran felt Todd was yet too negligent and irresponsible to fully undertake his responsibility of taking care of his daughter.

As no relief to her apprehension and fears of Todd's irresponsible traits, one night when calling, the phone was answered by a strange voice. It was a man's voice. The voice stated that Todd was not home, that Eara was there.

Immediately, Fran responded, "Oh, my god!!! Who are you and what are you doing there?"

The voice never answered, but decided to turn away and echoed as it was handing the phone to Todd, "Brother, you better answer this call. It sounds like some old mean busybody heifer on the other end!"

As Todd answered the phone, he realized that it was his mother Fran on the other end and he immediately chastised the voice person, "Be careful what you say when the phone is off the hook! And, don't be calling my mother a heifer!"

The voice responded, "I am sorry, man, I didn't know it was your mother. She didn't identify herself."

Todd replied, "Let's let this go this time." He then very adamantly replied to Fran, "That was a friend who answered the phone. He has just recently returned from Europe and is temporarily staying in the apartment with us."

Naturally. Fran became concerned again and apprehensive about Eara's welfare and wellness, living in an apartment with two men.

As time passed, Todd had now moved into his "new" girlfriend's apartment. However, this did not last long for their relationship soon ended. So Todd rented another apartment for he and Eara to live in. These were difficult times for Todd. So much so that (as Fran's friend Gloria

Burgess reported after visiting certain family members in New York) Todd would take Eara to the theatre during working hours and was making a feeble attempt to care for her.

To add insult to injury, in November of 1979, Todd had to travel to Europe to perform a part in a movie, and, therefore he sent Eara back to her mother. When Fran learned of Todd's situation (knowing the conditions under which the child was living and still feeling both parents were totally irresponsible), she pleaded with him (as she had done several times before) to bring/send the child to Dayton, to be with her loving grandparents. She pleaded with Todd to bring/send Eara to be with she and Jess until he could afford a responsible housekeeper/full-time baby sitter for Eara. Once again and as always Todd refused. This rejection irritated Fran very much.

Yet, Fran, in the spirit of enduring LOVE, kept the faith. She realized that there was nothing she could do once Eara was sent back to Andrea.

However, approximately six months later when Fran was attempting to keep in touch with her precious granddaughter, she learned that in April of 1980, Andrea left New York, stating that she was going to Texas in order to take care of her ailing mother (Deborah Louise Roberts Hall).

Her mother was eighty years old, like Jethro, and had experienced a lifetime full of joy and happiness. She rarely complained and handled life's issues one day at a time. Unknowingly to her mother, this was becoming a time of reuniting the family. During the same month Andrea's sister, Lee, also had moved from New York to live in Texas, along with the other sister, Tina and her six brats.

When Fran finally made contact with Andrea, to

avoid imminent confrontation, Andrea sidetracked Fran and allegedly reported to Fran that Tina was a poorly kept mother on welfare and an alcoholic, who from time to time suffered from bouts of schizophrenia. Yet Andrea, who was laden with so many faults like everyone else in society, left Eara with Jethro, her father. Her father was now eighty years old and living alone in New York. What was going through Andrea's mind? Did she think her six-and-one-half-year-old daughter was capable enough to take care of an eighty-year-old man? Did she think an eighty-year-old man was adequately capable to take care of a six-and-one-half-year-old girl? Did she think she could avoid the moment of truth?

The answer to all of the questions was no. When Fran was finally made aware of Eara's whereabouts, she immediately called Jethro. When communicating with him, she learned that it was difficult for him to comb Eara's hair, care for her and send her to school. Fran's only response to all this was, "This is insaneness; utter stupidity. This is utterly repugnant to the resurgence of feminine pride and upward mobility."

While Fran was concerned about the insaneness that was going on in New York, at this time, Andrea's mother, Andrea, the sisters and the grandchildren, all of them lived in a large apartment house. The apartment house was in very poor condition and Andrea's intentions were to try to fix up the house and to stay in Texas. However, the mother deceased in May of 1980. Thus Jethro and his son, William Isaiah Hall, and Eara all journeyed to Texas. This trip was not only to honor the beloved departed but also so that the Jethro can be relieved of his familial responsibilities (which he was no longer able to do) and give them back to Andrea to take care of her own daughter.

When making a continued attempt to learn more about the continuing sagas of Eara's welfare, Fran called Jethro, while he was in Texas. Instead of immediately addressing the Eara issue, he told her, "Deborah didn't own that large apartment house and after her death the real owner told us all to get out. All of us are now moving from pillar to post. Some nights if William and I are lucky we get a room at the St. Vincent DePaul Shelter for the homeless. Other than that we live on the street. As far as the girls are concerned, I am not sure where they and Eara are living. Most of the time it's one place or another for a short period of time. I think, but I am not sure, they are presently living in a run-down house on C Street. According to William, I believe Andrea has a job working at night and sometimes she uses her twenty-six year-old, retarded nephew to baby sit Eara. And, by word of mouth from Lee, I heard that Andrea, at other times, would lock Eara in the house and leave her there alone, while exploring a life in the streets. I really feel sad for Eara. Andrea should be ashamed of herself. What she is doing is not the way to properly raise up a child."

After hearing all of this unfavorable gossip about Andrea from her family members, Fran was beside herself with anger, depression, frustration and worry.

Further complicating matters for Fran, sometime in June, July or August of 1980, she was not doing well physically. She had undergone left hip replacement surgery. So Eara did not visit with her Ohio grandparents during the summer of 1980. It was decided, however, that by Christmas of 1980, Fran would probably be better and Eara could visit then. In addition, Todd said if necessary, he would come home during the holidays (the festive season) in order to help with Eara's care.

Sometime after Thanksgiving of 1980, Fran was able

to locate motor mouth Lee, Andrea's sister and Fran's bosom buddy friend from their very first meeting. When asked, she told Fran that Eara had no winter coat to wear and suggested that one be purchased for Eara, before coming to Ohio for Christmas.

Eara was to arrive on Christmas Eve; however, she was not on the plane when it arrived in Dayton. As usual Fran got very upset and called Lee again concerning Eara's whereabouts. Lee's reply to Fran was, "I don't know what kind of funny business Andrea is trying to accomplish, but she and Eara left early during the day of Christmas Eve, supposedly going to the airport. Neither of them has been seen by any of Andrea's close friends or anyone else."

Nonetheless, Eara finally arrived in Dayton on the evening of Christmas day. She called her grandparents. When Fran and Jess arrived to pick her up, Fran still steaming with rage and frustration, took her anger out on seven-year-old Eara. The only response teary-eyed Eara could muster up was, "Mommy messed up and we spent the night in a motel near the airport in Houston, Texas. So mommy was able to make arrangements to board me on planes to Atlanta and Dayton early this morning."

After arriving at the grandparents' home, Fran and Eara went to her beautiful, clean, well-kept room to unpack her ragged little brown bag. It contained only one pair of panties, two pair of Andrea's socks, an old faded dress (which Eara received in October for her birthday) and a new skirt, which was so small Eara couldn't wear it.

Having already known and understood what her grandchild was enduring, Fran lovingly endured her pain. However, to ease the child's pain, Fran supposedly had already finished her Christmas shopping for Eara and had bought her quite a few clothes. She unwrapped them in Eara's presence not only to see the wide expression of joy and thankfulness on Eara's face but also to let Eara know she now has much more to wear than what she brought with her.

Shortly after getting Eara settled in, Todd arrived on the same evening, looking very exquisitely dressed. However, he brought no gifts for his child.

Naturally Fran lashed out. "You've come home looking all flashy, GQ, and prosperous, but did you consider your only child's feelings and poverty-stricken conditions? You ought to be ashamed of yourself! What kind of father are you? Surely you were not raised to be the creature you've become!"

Looking Fran squarely in the eyes, Todd responded, "Woman, if I've told you once I've told you a thousand times, there are certain issues, you and I shall never discuss. I did not come home to listen to your lip service. I came home to see my baby girl. This is supposed to be the season of joy, so the two of you need to step aside so I can holler at my child."

At this juncture, Jess jumped to his feet and was ready to go to blows. However, Fran stepped in to bring that lasting and loving peace back into the household for Eara's sake.

The day following Christmas, Todd left in order to spend the remainder of the holiday season with his friends. On the other hand, on this same day (the biggest shopping spree day of the year), to fill in where her son miserably failed, Fran, showing compassionate love, took Eara shopping and bought a new coat and a new pair of shoes for her. The shoes that Eara arrived in were badly worn and much too large.

At the end of the Christmas break Fran and Jess took Eara to the Cincinnati, Ohio Northern Kentucky Airport to board a plane back to Texas. That was the last time she was heard from until April of 1981.

Every time Fran asked Todd if he had heard from Eara the answer was "no." After receiving so many "no" answers, Fran decided to call Jethro. The report from Jethro was equally as bad. Jethro reported, "Andrea called me some months ago, as a matter of fact in February of 1981, asking for some money because she was flat broke and she and Eara had no place to stay. Of course, I sent her enough money for them to come home, but I have not heard from them since February. Fran, I have nothing else to report. I only ask that you pray for my daughter and our precious 'baby' Eara."

Fran's heart, mind and soul almost gave up the Ghost after listening to Jethro's report and request. However, finding courage within to lovingly endure all things, Fran never gave up hope and continued to make several attempts to locate them, even though these attempts were in vain and by now the worry and anxiety were overwhelming.

In March of 1981, one morning while lying in bed and worrying about Eara, Fran's aging mind suddenly remembered the name of the school, which during one conversation Eara had mentioned she attended. It was Orville & Wilbur Wright Elementary.

It had to be God's answer to one of many of Fran's prayers, asking for guidance in locating the child. Hardly containing herself until the next morning, Fran arose early that morning. She called the school. God answered her prayer because the operator was able to contact the school and it was the right one. However, Fran was informed by the school that Eara had attended there but had been withdrawn from the school on January 12th,

1981 and that her mother had said that they were going to return to Indiana. (They never lived in Indiana.) The request as to whether anyone at the school could name another school where Eara may have been enrolled brought the reply, "No!" Additional response from the school's administration office stated, "Our records show Eara owes us $12.00 for a book she borrowed from our library and therefore we will not transfer any of her records."

Fran immediately thought, "Oh my God. This means Eara has not been in school from January until March. I will send the school a check to clear up the debt." Though, the check for a measly $12.00 was received as Fran learned when she called a week or so later, to her surprise, while hoping for more information to be forthcoming, the person answering the phone would not divulge any more information.

When LOVE endures, Fran realized this was not the time to get ugly and to start chastising others for the awful mistakes of a mother.

Having no luck with the school authorities concerning Eara's whereabouts, by now Fran was frantic, not knowing whether Eara was homeless, hungry or just where she could be. So she decided to call Jethro to inquire if he had heard any more from Andrea and Eara since February. He told Fran that they were there with him. Immediately Fran asked if she could speak with Andrea.

"What has been going on with you and my granddaughter since February of this year?"

Lying lips Andrea replied, "I have been in New York for three weeks. And, when my boyfriend came to get me, there was no room in his small, ragged, junk car for Eara. Therefore I left Eara here in Texas with one of my cousins. Eara is doing fine and I'll be leaving her here, again, with cousin Betty when I go back to New York." Fran, knowing by now how much a habitual and pathetic prevaricator Andrea has become, decided to find the truth by calling her old and trusted friend and comrade Lee. Lee told her that Eara had been left with Tina rather than with a cousin as Andrea had reported. Why all of this secrecy and cover-up concerning Eara's education, whereabouts, well-being and welfare? So much so that Jethro was shamefully caught in the middle!!!

Fran remembered the report from Andrea of the type of environment in which Tina lived, so she decided to pump Lee for more information, while she had the opportunity.

Lee told Fran, "Tina could hardly take care of her own six or seven children, as well as her own poor health and Welfare conditions. Most of the time Tina doesn't even know the whereabouts or even care about the education and welfare of her own brats. Plussss—all of Tina's brats constantly have been harassing Eara. From time to time they make her feel like a non-person by telling Eara she does not belong there and that she is going to end up 'a good for nothing' like her mother who often goes away and leaves her!"

With this information Fran immediately decided to call Todd. "Do you have any idea what has been going in your only daughter's life for the past three months? Do you really care, since you found it more benefiting to bond with your friends rather than with her at Christmas of last year?"

Todd, now getting upset, replied, "I have no idea what is going on in Eara's life."

Fran quipped, "Now that you have been informed what do you intend to do about it?"

Todd, as always being the high and mighty and concerned only about himself, retorted, "There is nothing I can do at the present time. As a matter of fact, you seem to be doing enough for all parties involved. Plusss—I am on my way to California. In a few days I'll be performing in a pilot for NBC Television."

Fran, becoming subtle and slightly irate at this point, responded, "If you do not do something about your only daughter's living conditions, education, well-being and welfare, I will take legal action to do so. The time has come and something needs to be done for my granddaughter and your only child!" On the latter response Todd hung up.

Having Eara subjected to the kind of abuse, environment, and mistreatment she was enduring while in Texas with Tina and her brats, hurt Fran terribly so. Fran often thought how terrible it must be for her precious granddaughter being neglected and perhaps being under emotional stress. As always out of empathetic and enduring LOVE, Fran made it a point to contact the Children's Services Bureau in Houston, Texas.

A voice replied, "We will investigate the matter, but in order to do so, the case would first have to be referred to the Children's Services Bureau in Dayton, Ohio."

However, after Fran discussed this matter with reliable persons at the Children's Services Bureau in Dayton, it was learned that in pursuing such a course of action, Eara might possibly end up in a foster home as a ward of the State.

Fran then consulted her attorney who advised her that since the parents were not divorced (who were supposedly never married, except by common law), custody of Eara had not been legally established. Therefore, with the father's permission, the grandmother could get temporary custody of Eara. For once Todd was on his mother's side. After Fran started initiating legal proceedings, Todd then obtained a legal document, from his attorney, confirming that his mother could have temporary custody of Eara and authorizing Lee to get Eara away from Tina and her brats.

However, all did not go as easily as was legally planned. In order to get Eara away from Tina and without the ugliness of Andrea's involvement, Lee knew that the children were going to attend an Easter egg hunt on Resurrection Sunday to be held at the Park Side Community Center, in Houston, Texas. Ceasing the right moment and opportunity, Lee picked Eara up at the egg hunt and put her on a plane bound for Ohio. She told Eara that she was going home to be with her loving grandparents.

Though Lee eventually received a tremendous amount of family flack for her involvement in Eara's rescue mission, Fran was very appreciative of her efforts. It was through this rescue mission that Fran (and Jess) was/were able to become the legal guardian(s)/custodian(s) of Eara as stated at the beginning of this story in chapter one.

In any event, when Fran and Jess met Eara at Dayton's Cox Airport, she was very sad. She was sad because:

- She didn't want to leave her little cousins in Texas although they had mistreated her.
- She thought she was coming to Ohio to live with her grandparents for only a few weeks and then once again she was going to be sent back to Texas to live (in those deplorable conditions) with her other family members.
- She could not understand why her mother had not

called and why she had not come after her. After all she so often heard her lying mother say, "I promise I'll come back to get you!"

Three weeks had passed and Andrea had not made any contact with Eara nor did she make an attempt to fulfill her promise.

Nonetheless, upon her arrival to her grandparents' home, it was discovered that the only clothes Eara had were those she was wearing. The couple of pieces her Aunt Lee had bought her, she was carrying them in a box. She was so tired that Fran undressed her. As she knelt beside the bed, Eara broke down and vehemently cried while she was whispering her prayers. Fran, empathetically feeling the child's enduring misery and pain, cried with her. Fran also cried because she had thought about how Eara had been so neglected. Fran cried because she was so happy that she had found Eara and brought her out of such a deplorable situation. Finally Fran put her into bed. Out of that enduring, loving sympathy for the child, Fran did not insist upon Eara taking a bath that night, although Eara very badly needed to take a bath. Her body odor was awful!

The next morning when bathing her, Fran noticed and observed that Eara's body was so unclean that the water in the tub was layered with scum. Fran also realized a shower was necessary in order to get Eara's skin clean. Her ankles, elbows, knees and the soles of her feet had been so neglected that a bath brush was necessary to unloose the cracked, dry, peeling skin. This was the only way to get those parts of her body clean. Her hair was equally as dirty and very long and thick and so tangled, it became an almost all morning task untangling the knots. Realizing how long it was taking Fran to clean her hair and body, from head to feet, Eara explained to Fran that her cousin, one of Tina's brats, did not always do a good job when combing her hair and that Tina's home had no hot water and no electricity.

It was now Palm Sunday 1981 and Eara had finally been able to tell Fran and Jess about the Easter Play that was in process at her school. This was the first revelation by Eara of ever being anywhere near a school, since her mother took her out of Orville & Wilbur Wright Elementary School. The only explanation one can rationalize is that, apparently Tina found out the custody case was under review. Tina, therefore, must have enrolled her into a school (whichever school it was that Eara attended since the family never divulged that information, nor were the circumstances surrounding that situation ever mentioned).

The latter does not matter now that Eara is under the watchful, all bearing and enduring loving care of Fran and Jess. Fortunately, the week of Eara's arrival, the Dayton schools were out for spring break. This provided time to begin making arrangements for Eara to attend a local school. However, because Fran and Jess had not the experience of having a child in school for 40 years, they found out there were many changes in the system about which they had not become aware. Yet with the help of friends, they became familiar with some of the rules and regulations and school policies. In particular, one of the first issues that Fran undertook was to obtain the necessary court's permission before entering Eara into school. This led to the realization that, after Eara's arrival, there were still many, many, many other issues to be resolved other than providing an adequate and sound academic growth area for Eara.

In fact, for all parents and grandparents alike, providing an adequate and sound education for one's child is not the only important issue that arises when dealing with today's youth. In this day and time, for many parents and grandparents, there are an unsurmountable number of issues that arise when dealing with today's youth and teenagers. Other important issues that surface when being involved with youth means dealing with youth: depression, discipline, eating habits, emotional feelings, freedom and space options, getting homework done, health and peer pressure issues, sleeping disorders, hanging out and becoming part of the "in-crowd" issue, making fashion statements and looking good issues, growing up in poverty and rat-infested homes, incest and child molestation, domestic violence, lack of spiritual upbringing, just to name a few.

Fortunately, for Fran and Jess, other than the academic issue, the immediate youth issues they had to deal with, concerning Eara, were bedtime disciple and providing acceptable clothing so Eara did not appear poverty-stricken when seen by the public.

Not being accustomed to going to bed at a certain time every night, Eara cried. And, whenever she cried, Eara expressed loneliness for her mommy. Apparently, no matter how terribly neglectful Andrea had become of her seven-and-one-half-year-old daughter, Eara still loved and longed to see her mother. This behavior was analogous to David's in Psalm 42:1. "As the heart panted after the water brooks, so panted my soul after thee, O God." Eara's young soul panted for more attention from her addicted, dope-filled, estranged, streetwise mother, who left her only child at this time comfortless and lonely to fend for herself. It was no wonder she cried every night. But thank God for a crying, loving and praying grandmother! It became a regular thing for Fran to get into bed with her and comfort her. Yet many times Fran was at a loss for words. After a few weeks, the crying began to lessen a bit, but it seemed that just when she would think Eara was adjusting, Eara would break down into another spell of crying. It took a heart consumed with enduring LOVE to get a child through the torment of a cold and neglectful mother's heartbreak.

To move Eara's young soul from sadness and loneliness to joy, the following week Fran took Eara shopping for a new Easter outfit. This occasion brought smiles on her face and heavenly delight and enjoyment into Eara's life. In addition Fran took Eara and one of her Dayton Ohio cousins, Regina King, to the Ice Follies on Good Friday afternoon. Eara and Regina bonded very soon after meeting and seemed to enjoy the Ice Follies show. As a matter of fact, Regina spent the entire weekend with Eara. On Saturday the two of them went to an Easter egg hunt at Wayman Chapel A.M.E. Church. Eara became brave and bold enough to sing in the youth choir on Resurrection Sunday morning. Eara had found new grace and appeared to be happy doing all the things that were inwardly and silently turning her life around.

On the Monday morning following the Easter weekend experiences, Fran had enrolled Eara into one of the local schools. Eara had some problems with reading and math. Fran frantically worried about solving this for her precious granddaughter. A light turned on in her head and she called her friend Laura Trayvik to save the day. Laura was a blue-eyed, petite, dainty and beautiful woman, who possessed soft and wavy hair and one who had a dual teaching degree in language arts and math. Laura tutored and worked with Eara so that she could catch up with the rest of her class. After all, having been out of school from January until March and now April, Eara had academically lost quite a bit.

Transportation to and from school was by the bus that picked-up and dropped-off Eara and other children, about one half block from the grandparents' home. Eara soon became friends with several of the other children who lived on the same street where Fran and Jess lived. They walked to the bus line together. As an "All-State" grandmother, ensuring her granddaughter was watched over and in dependent and secure hands, Fran always stood on the porch looking down the street to witness that all was well with Eara and the other children. She would wave to Eara as she boarded the bus. In the evening after returning home from school, Eara and her newfound friends would get together and play games until it became suppertime followed by homework time followed by bedtime.

By now, Eara had also met many other friends at school and through the Young People's Department at the Church. The Young People's Department provided many activities through which all youth could socially and spiritually bond, develop, grow and nurture. Eara was adjusting well in her present Dayton, Ohio environment. Within this context, one of her newly acquainted friends was Yolanda Byrd, who lived in Jefferson Township, the southwest suburb of Dayton where bike riding was safer. And, as soon as the spring season of 1981 arrived, Jess or Yolanda's grandfather would take Eara's bike to this suburb so the two of them could safely play, ride, and talk kid stuff. In addition, from late spring season down to the first snow in the fall season, Fran took Eara and Yolanda to many carnivals and amusement parks.

Another newly acquainted friend was Nikki Wilt.

They attended a children's theatre during the summer months of 1981. Fran as well as the two of them enjoyed making their costumes and the practicing for the show that was given at the end of the season. Eara and Nikki became even closer friends as they shared a room at the "Y" camp, which was sponsored each summer.

When the spring, summer and fall seasons' activities ceased, Eara was given new opportunities to participate in indoor winter season activities. Her Aunt Bert, Fran's sister, gave Eara a gift of a pair of roller skates. On Saturday afternoons Eara usually went skating, either at the Roller Rink on Hoover Avenue in Dayton, Ohio or on Brown School Road in Vandalia, Ohio, with the other youth of the church and/or the youth from the street on which she now lived.

By providing such a gift and an indoor winter season opportunity, Eara came to very much appreciate and love her short, sassy, ageless, forever tanned, youthful Aunt Bert.

Bike riding, camping out and roller skating were not the only new activities of joy and well-being that were introduced in Eara's new life style. For Eara, Nikki, Yolanda and the other youth at the church there was always a program on holidays and on the Saturday preceding Halloween. Thus, these young women would have a sleepover party and then have breakfast together, at the grandparent's home(s), before attending Sunday school and the Sunday Morning Worship Service.

It is obvious that Fran and Jess tried the very best that they could accomplish to keep Eara as busy as humanly possible, as she seemed to be very happy after a few months in Ohio. To add sugar and spice to her home life, in her room she had her own television, tape player, and all the pretty little girl things to make her comfortable. She took great pride in showing her room to her little friends. Often she mentioned how proud she was to have her own room. "Grams and Grampa, it was never like this in New York or Texas. I thank you both for such blessings and I am very proud of the both of you and my own rooooom. No more sharing and sleeping in dingy rooms on cots or the floor, with strangers or bad ass cousins. Both of you have made me very, very, very happy."

During this period of re-adjustment, Eara also spent much time with Aunt Bert (her official baby sitter and new mentor). They enjoyed playing children's card games (like go fish) and going places together. This new bonding with Aunt Bert was excellent and timely because it was now October of 1981 and two life-changing events were on the precipice of taking place in her young life. One, Fran had to have her second hip replacement surgery, and, therefore was unable to attend to Eara's needs, as she was accustomed to doing. Hence, Fran had to leave all such matters of taking care of Eara, in the hand of her devoted and loving husband Jess and to her trusted sisters, while she was recuperating in the hospital. Two, on October 17, 1981 Eara would become a womanish eight-year-old going on twenty-eight.

And for this precious eight-year-old going on twenty-eight, life is full of irony. Isn't it ironic? Andrea did not call Eara or try to contact her until her eighth birthday on October 17, 1981. Andrea had the audacity to tell Fran, while on her sick bed, that she had heard and (falsely) understood (perhaps from Eara not wanting her mother to feel guilty of neglect) that Eara was unhappy living there (at the grandparents' home). Sick or not, Fran suddenly found grace, surely goodness and mercy within to sit up and say to Andrea, "May God have mercy and forgiveness on your sick soul and twisted mind. Eara is doing well. And, another thing, I for one disapproved of your motherly behavior and instincts and you ought to be ashamed of yourself for abandoning the child."

On the latter remark, Andrea hung up the phone, and on this occasion, she did not ask for Eara to be returned to her nor did she offer any further explanation concerning her actions of neglect and mistreatment of her daughter.

So we have seen, in this chapter of Eara's young life (that through the acts of Eara's grandparents, the acts of her beloved family members and friends and in particular the action of Fran) that when LOVE endures all, LOVE, not only suffers long, but also LOVE:

- Is kind.
- Does not hold envy over the mundane.
- Is not boastful or braggadocio.
- Is not puffed up.
- Is compassionate and reaches out to the downtrodden, something Andrea and Todd will hopefully come to realize as they reach life's maturity.

Three
When Love Conquers All

When LOVE conquers all LOVE has the power to show nothing can separate God and humanity. LOVE has the power to show nothing can separate endearing grandparents and their granddaughter or any other grandchildren. This type of LOVE has the power to show no trial or tribulation can break one's spirit. This type of LOVE has the power to find joy in a sea of hate, joy in sorrow, joy in sickness, and joy in broke-ness and brokenness. This type of LOVE has the power to find peace in the middle of a storm and comfort in the middle of a living death. When LOVE conquers all LOVE has the power to show, with the Master's stubbornness, it can overcome any adversity or threat in life.

In this chapter, let us see how such exemplary LOVE was shown again and again (by Eara's grandparents particularly by Fran, as well as by other family members and friends) as Eara's life moved through seasons of more disappointment, challenge, melancholy, pain and sickness to seasons of joy, from eight years old to her preteen adolescence.

In early December of 1981, Eara had a bout with pneumonia, which made it difficult for Fran to take care of her so soon after surgery. By the hidden hand of Grace, Fran managed to take Eara to and from the doctor's office and the hospital until Eara recovered. Getting up with Eara during the nights was difficult. Many nights Eara rested more comfortably when Fran would get into bed with her. Every evening after coming in from school, while Fran was resting, Eara would climb upon the bed with her and the two of them would sing their favorite songs.

Sometime about the middle of December of 1981, Todd had called saying he would be home for Christmas. Eara was looking forward to having a great time with her father. Eara had told her schoolmates that her dad, the actor, would be home for Christmas. Eara's entire family and friends were all looking forward to this visit. It was the first time Eara and all would get the chance to see him since May of 1981.

As always, when it came to Eara and the family, Todd would never keep his appointed time of arrival. He arrived several days later following Christmas and brought gifts with him. Todd probably reflected back on the tongue-lashing he got a year ago for coming home, looking all distinguished, and without any gifts for Eara. So he probably decided not to make the same mistake. However, he was not aware a day or two before his arrival a lady from Philadelphia called asking if Eara's gifts from her dad had arrived. Thus upon his arrival Eara, Fran and Jess did not act surprised at his "bragging" about the gifts he brought with him. More importantly all dismissed Todd's "flaunting behavior" because it was later learned that the lady from Philadelphia supplied the money for Eara's gifts and most of Eara's Christmas gifts had already been purchased by her grandparents.

Fran not being one to let an opportunity slip by (particularly when it came to gathering information regarding her son), she quickly seized the moment to become acquainted with the lady from Philadelphia. After meeting by phone, they talked many times, somewhat at length, regarding she and Todd's relationship.

It was during this Christmas season visit when many noticeable changes had taken place in Todd's personality. He cried often. He had mood swings. He had bouts of depression. One morning about 3 A.M. he was heard, in the basement, walking the floor and beating his fists together and against the walls.

The basement was an apartment and it was somewhat cooler there than in the upper rooms of Fran and Jess' home. Todd chose to sleep in the basement and while there he also drank to excess. It was a good choice for him to be in the basement since Eara was not completely over her bout with pneumonia. It was equally important for Todd to abide in the basement since Fran really began to notice a drastic change in his behavior, at this time. However, out of yearning to be with her undevoted father, Eara wold sneak down to the basement to see him, although she was repeatedly told to stay upstairs. This disobedience really got to Fran.

"Eara, if I've told you once I've told you a thousand times, do not go down to the basement in your condition to be with that loose cannon you worship as a father. Come upstairs and go to your room at once!"

"But grandma, I just want to see what is wrong with him and if he needed some medicine or something."

"Never mind what he needs, get upstairs at once."

"But grandma, he is really ill or something. Maybe we need to take him to the doctor."

"Child, don't make me have to come down there and drag you up those steps."

"But grandma, his hands are bleeding. Could we treat his wounds to stop the bleeding?"

"Child, have you lost your mind? Oh, Lord, Jess hand me your belt. I've got to whip some sense in this child's head, if she does not mind me this instant."

On this last response from Fran, Eara hastened upstairs. Simultaneously, Todd, becoming very hostile and angry, shouted from the basement:

"Woman what in the name of Satan is wrong with you? What in the name of Lucifer did you think I was going to do to my daughter? Why are you suspicious of me?"

Todd's behavior had so drastically changed, that Fran and Jess found it a relief when he left for Philadelphia and/or New York a few days later. It did not make any difference to them. They were glad he was gone!

Yet, Todd was not done with his parents. In fact, a few weeks later, he called and asked if Eara could visit him in New York, during spring break.

Reluctant to give permission, Fran silently held the phone and did not say yea or nay. After a few minutes she finally said, "Let's discuss this issue sometime later." And, she hung up the phone.

Todd, becoming very hostile, immediately called back and said, "If I come to get my kid and you won't let me have her, you'll be sorry!"

This was too shocking for Fran, so she just quietly hung up the phone, again.

Fran was so shocked at her son's devastating behavior, the only thing she could do at that moment was to go to her bedroom, get on top of her bed linen and rest there with a cold compress on her forehead. This really worried Jess to see Fran in this condition so much so that he wanted to call Todd back and give him a manly piece of what was on his mind. However, Jess being the man of God that he is, he conquered his feelings and bridled his tongue for Fran's sake. However, Jess' actions did not keep Fran from thinking, "What kind of a fool son did I spawn? His child was getting the very best care, the best of everything. Why would such an insolent and disrespectful fool make such a threat to his mother?"

To allay her fears, the next day when contacting the Juvenile Court, Fran was informed that she was responsible for Eara, that she had custody of Eara and that if Todd caused any trouble, she was to immediately notify the police.

Thus, began an unfavorable communication bridge over troubled waters between beloved mother and son. In particular, Todd developed a series of "favorable-unfavorable" attitudes. One day he would call and say how very grateful he was for the excellent care being given to Eara. The next week he would call, hostile and sarcastic, and accuse Fran of trying to alienate the child from him. Many times he called sobbing and crying and his behavior was so erratic and irrational that it was not even considered feasible to allow Eara to talk to him. Many times his calls were person to person in order to ignore his mother and get straight to his daughter. Yet, even Eara began to notice that her father had a problem. Within this context, Fran and Jess never spoke of her parents' neglect nor did they say anything unkindly or unfavorable of them to Eara. As far as Eara was concerned, she was with her grandparents because her parents had no proper home for raising her. And, as the evidence proved again and again, they didn't.

As a matter of fact, in regards to the latter statement, Andrea, by this time, was living with her boyfriend in, what has been allegedly reported as, a run-down shack in a very poverty-stricken neighborhood. Her father was living in Harlem, New York, in what according to Fran's attorney, by investigation, was a very deplorable location.

Meanwhile back on the scene in Dayton, Ohio, above and beyond all that has been penned thus far, in September of 1982, Eara was promoted to third grade and was in Woodrow Wilson Magnet School. After Fran explained all of the circumstances surrounding her custody and guardianship of Eara to the principal of the school, he was very understanding. Arrangements were made such that Eara was not to be released at any time from the school to anyone but Fran or Jess.

By this time, Eara was adjusting very well. Very often close contact was maintained with her teachers for any sign of emotional change(s). All reports from them were favorable. Eara received average grades and made many friends in school. Concerning the average grades, the grandparents accepted but gently pushed for continuous improvement and achievement. In addition to academics, Eara showed she inherited and possessed other talents. She was playing flute in the school band and was very much interested in music. In other extracurricular settings, she undertook organ lessons, but didn't show much interest in this aspect of instrumental music. Nonetheless, Eara found her niche in another instrumental field and she appeared to be a very talented flutist.

In terms of further aspirations or endeavors or involvements in the musical field, Eara then respectively joined the school choir and the junior choir in the church. With encouragement from Fran and others, she began to accompany the junior choir on the flute. Inasmuch as she appeared to be enjoying and excelling in certain aspects of the musical field, it was discovered that she really had to be motivated to hold interest in certain things. With further encouragement and some persuasion from Fran, after her fourth school year, Eara was enrolled in a music seminar, for nine weeks during the summer of 1983, which she thoroughly enjoyed. Out of the latter context, Eara was placed in the advanced band session at school and that become very challenging for her.

She enjoyed this challenge, as well as many of life's other academic, economical, political, social and survival challenges. She also enjoyed being popular. She even made an attempt to run for President of the Student Council.

Yet, there was one challenge that was not a concern to Eara. It was her increasing obesity. Eara's grandparents always provided plenty of food. In so doing, she was never denied anything she wanted to eat. And during this period, Eara unfortunately gained "some" weight. However, she didn't seem to care too much about such an obesity issue at this time. Her reaction to her weight gain was not too much different than many young females at her age. Paralleling whatever thoughts Eara had on this subject, Fran and Jess felt that due to the fact that she had not always had sufficient food, this habit of eating would soon pass and thereby her weight would lessen. Fran further discussed the issue with her doctor. Eara's doctor didn't seem too concerned and felt that she would lose the weight during her teen years. Naturally, Todd blamed Fran for her weight gain.

Apparently, at this stage of her pre-ten-year-old life, other lifetime interaction challenges arose. Eara began to develop other human faults and frailties other than her weight gain. As time passed, Eara began to become a bit womanish. She began to become a bit arrogant and was becoming a bit determined to have her way. Fran had to employ that conquering LOVE spirit sooner than she thought.

"Young lady, as long as you are under our roof, we want you to always remember we love you. But that arrogant behavior, showing us the hand, sashaying off when we are speaking to you and attempting to have your way all the time shall not be tolerated at all!!! Do you clearly understand me?"

"But Grams, I love you too and your thoughts are not always my thoughts and they are not always right."

"Yes, what you say may be true *at times* but grandmother is older and wiser and knows best. There are just certain things your grandfather and I will not tolerate. Are we clear on these matters?"

"Yes, mamma."

"Now that's a good girl."

Fran was always happy when she and Eara could reason together and lovingly work out their differences. Part of this quick resolution process was due to Fran's understanding nature. She always empathetically and sympathetically put herself in Eara's shoes and so often thought that Eara was maybe experiencing a bit of depression at times. And, to conquer those occurrences of depression, Fran would graciously and lovingly allow Eara to call her grandfather Jethro in New York, who she called "Pop, Pop." These call allowances usually made Eara feel much better, although she seldom talked about her mommy in the process.

Other than becoming a bit arrogant and a bit determined to have her way and going through bouts of depression, also at this stage of her young life, Eara became very sensitive and it didn't take much to make her cry. Consequently Fran learned not to raise her voice in correcting or disciplining her. Eara could take being corrected, but when Fran raised her voice she became very nervous. Eara would cry easily and yet simultaneously speak what was on her mind, while in tears. Later this became a very convenient weapon Eara used often, since she was one to have the last word. However, Fran had to find a way to use that loving conquering spirit to swiftly change Eara's "having the last word attitude." That attitude had to be changed.

In most cases when Fran firmly and persuasively said, "Case closed," she was as serious as a heart attack. Fran was not playing and Eara, therefore, ceased to talk back.

One day a light turned on in her faculties and Eara said, "Grams, I am beginning to understand you now." With those words, a new line of communication seemed to open up. Here after when Eara responded to Fran with "Grams," Fran realized she was able to discipline Eara and correct her without Eara thinking Fran was angry with her. In fact, Eara didn't want "Grams" to ever be angry with her and would do almost anything to prevent it.

Once the home front issues were resolved between granddaughter and grandmother, there were yet other challenges that Fran had to undertake, at her age.

In August of 1983, Todd called saying that he was in the hospital having suffered a spinal stroke as a result of an accident. He also mentioned that in order not to become a paraplegic, he had undergone surgery. His surgeon called and confirmed what he had told the family.

Being the ever forgiving and loving mother (with that indwelling conquering spirit to win over her son to change his ways to become a more caring, dependable, devoted, loving and responsive and responsible father, even though he was now somewhat incapacitated), before the beginning of the school in September, Fran and Bert took Eara to New York to see her now crippled dad. Although he was recuperating in a therapeutic hospital for therapy, Todd came to the hotel where they were staying. He hired a limousine and took the three of them out to dinner and to a Broadway show.

Such an expression of love, by Todd, touched Fran very much. Yet, for her, it became very depressing to see and note Todd's crippled right hand, leg and back, although he was able to get around. It also became apparent and quite obvious that Todd was definitely not acting normal. Fran perhaps hoped the ultimate change was on the way as a result of Todd's current predicament and circumstances. Yet her greatest concern was whether it was safe or not safe to allow him to take Eara to see her little cousins who lived in New York.

In any event, when the three of them were about to depart for the return trip to Dayton, Ohio, Todd appeared very sad and Eara cried for hours. Was Todd sad because (before their departure) he had given his mother $600.00 to help support Eara or was he sad because, for once in his life, he realized he is really going to miss his precious little girl? Only time will tell.

Nevertheless, as soon as Fran got back to Dayton, she deposited the $600.00 into an interest bearing savings account for Eara's future. She and Jess were thankful that God always provided and they never had an occasion to withdraw any of Eara's support money for whatever reason.

After having undertaken the challenge of the father daughter reunion, Fran's next challenge was to see to it that all of Eara's school's academic and social concerns were in place and being properly implemented, once Eara was again enrolled in school in September. Although it wasn't always easy, Fran attended as many school meetings as possible. She attended the programs, the band concerts, the choir performances, and whatever else parents were expected to attend. It was often amusing to see

Fran climbing the steps to the school's entrance, holding on to the rails that were made for children. Somehow Fran also provided the necessary amount of income and supplies Eara needed to participate in trips.

As a matter of fact, sometime in October of 1983, the school sponsored a trip to Washington, D.C. for the students and Eara had a great time on that trip. It was a wonderful experience for her. She talked about the trip for weeks thereafter.

All of the above and this joyful trip were not the only memorable life-changing events in Eara's young existence, since arriving in Dayton, Ohio in April of 1981. On her 10th birthday, October 17th 1983, Eara had a sleepover and invited three of her closest friends. The three of them had quite a time. The following morning, Fran and Jess took all of them to a Pancake House for breakfast.

Two plus years have passed since Eara, Fran and Jess became a family. Within that time frame the family was doing well. Eara was very happy and Fran had never had an occasion of discipline or rude behavior which warranted spanking her. However, shortly after Eara came she showed Fran a mark on her back, which Eara said had been made by Andrea whipping her with a belt and the buckle left the mark.

"Oh, baby girl, you have been scarred for life. I promise, from this moment, no matter what misbehavior or wrongdoing you shall possibly commit, I will never use such disciplinary or corrective action measures. Do you understand what I am saying to you?"

"Oh, yes, Grams, and I dearly thank you for such consideration. I love you."

"I love you too."

However, Eara being the budding, inquisitive, young

woman she was becoming, a few weeks later after the "understanding exchange," Fran found her reading an obscene note from one of her schoolmates. Fran attempted to take it from her. Eara resisted. The wrestling match for the note ensued. In the course of action, Fran stuck Eara with her right thumbnail, which left a small scratch on Eara's left hand. The result of the wrestling match shamed one party and badly hurt the pride of the other party, so much so, that there was never another problem with a similar situation.

Shortly thereafter, other problems began to surface. One day when inquiring about homework, Fran found out Eara (like many children her age who become academically challenged or lazy) began to lie about performing her homework. She would hide it and say she didn't have any to do. In fact, actually she did have several assignments. Fran also found out, Eara had been intercepting some progress reports, which the school had mailed to the grandparents' home. And, later in this regard, Fran also found out Eara's academic work began to show some unfavorable grades.

Out of this context, Fran realized it was time to conquer imminent failure. Conquering LOVE action stepped up to the plate. Fran decided to assist Eara with all of her assignments every evening. By this action, it was soon discovered that Eara began to become dependent upon Fran's help. However, on the contrary, Fran encouraged and taught her how to do more of the assignments on her own. Eara's grades began to improve somewhat and one semester she made the all-city honor roll, of which she seemed to be quite proud. This didn't last too long however, and although promoted at the end of the year, Eara's grades were not as good as they should or could have been.

Visiting the school and talking with the teachers, all of them agreed that Eara had the ability but seemed to have lost interest in school. Was this academic fallout due to her early upbringing?

Fran realized corrective and special attention was needed to arrest the imminent academic failure problem. Hence Fran respectively approached the ever-negligent parents, Todd and Andrea, (especially money bags, slick actor Todd) with the idea of sending Eara to a boarding or parochial or private school. Naturally both of them sadly objected. At this point, Fran wanted to know from the entire earthly universe, are there any other parents out there as pitiful as these two?

Yet on the side of good news/bad news, sometime after Thanksgiving of 1983, Todd called and said that he felt he would be released from the hospital in order to spend Christmas with the family. The family was happy to hear this news, although Fran had her reservations about his coming. However, for the sake of the child, she relented and somewhat even looked forward to Todd's coming home for Christmas. Secretly, Fran hoped that by Christmas time Todd would have overcome his drinking habit, inasmuch as he always denied that he had one.

On the other hand, Eara was excited that her dad was coming home for Christmas. Why? She was excited because the school band was planning a Christmas Programme on December 15, 1983 commencing at 7 P.M. Her dad had never seen or heard her perform or play her favorite instrument. Eara even took her excitement a step further into the trust factor. She told all her schoolmates about her dad, and he promised to autograph her closest friend's notebooks. Todd had faithfully promised to be in attendance and all evening long Eara watched for him. As usual Todd did not show up. Here was a man and a father who just could not live up to his word. One often wonders if Todd ever realized his word was his covenant and when one breaks one's covenant one might as well forget ever being believed or trusted again. This action on Todd's part was a great disappointment for Eara.

Later that night he arrived at his parents' home after all the musical festivities, the fellowshipping and the dining out were over. As always, Todd had an alibi. Thank God for a compassionate, devoted, ever loving, faithful and forgiving daughter. She was learning from her grandmother conquering LOVE allows one to become the bigger person and therefore allows one to forgive another of her or his human faults and frailties. So Eara graciously acquiesced his alibi.

Nonetheless, Fran observed that Todd did not drink quite as much at this time compared with his previous home visits. In defense of his lessened drinking habit, Todd stated that his doctor had prescribed Valium and Percocet for his pain.

Todd's drinking habit, while taking prescription medication, did not concern him very much. His greater concern at the time was not having the full attention and relationship with his daughter as he had expected and hoped. From Fran's vantage point (judging by the accusatory remarks he would make from time to time), it appeared that Todd seemed to be resentful of the relationship. As a matter of fact he was absolutely jealous of the relationship, which had been established between Eara and her grandparents. From Todd's vantage point, it appeared that Eara seemed to pay more attention to the grandparents than to her father. If Todd were a wise man, he should not have expected as comfortable a relationship with him as it were with her grandparents. Did he momentarily forget? After all, he has been the absentee, neglectful, nonattentive, non-bonding, non-caring, non-present, non-supportive father for the last ten years.

By early January of 1984, Todd came to himself and realized under the circumstances his best option was to leave without much ado. As a matter of fact, his real reason for leaving at this time was that he was able to resume working. Later in the spring, he reported that he had been called to California to make another pilot for NBC Television.

Somewhere between the January and Spring time frame, Todd called and requested $500.00 of the money he had given to Fran, during the time of their visit to New York to help with Eara's support. Todd's call sounded urgent and Fran, not having that amount of money on hand at that instant, got up out of her "easy chair" and hastened to the bank and withdrew $300.000 from Eara's savings account and sent it to him, via Western Union Money Express. During this entire process, Fran thought to herself, "What kind of a father gives and takes back what little support he has given to his only daughter?"

In addition to the latter call, Todd called often during his work assignment in California. What were his ultimate reasons for calling often, at this time? And, as per his previous calling M.O., they were person-to-person calls to Eara in hopes of avoiding talking to Fran. Perhaps, he often attempted not to hear Fran's voice on the other end of the line because he was aware that she was able to tell when he was under the influence. He was not up to hearing another lecture from her on any occasion. Although the latter may have infrequently occurred, Fran never refused to allow Eara to talk with her father. Fran's only stipulations were that:

- Todd's conversation not to make any statements in conflict with what she was attempting to teach Eara, in terms of being trained up in the way a child should go.
- Todd must not be too incoherent when conversing, if he were under the influence.

Although Todd called several times, Andrea seldom called.

In moving forward, Fran continued to find ways to conquer and leap over the alleged negative effects Todd was attempting to introduce into Eara's upward thinking and mobility. Through that ever-present conquering LOVE bond, Eara and her grandmother had grown very close. They had grown more understanding of each other. As Eara began to express herself more freely and would disagree at times, Fran felt she had won Eara's respect and confidence.

Each morning, when getting Eara up for school, Fran would sit on her bed and say, "God bless you, Baby." Each morning they had breakfast together and during these quality times Eara would tell Fran how much she loved her. And further, Eara never left for school without each of them saying, "I love you" to each other. One morning when they were rushing and didn't take the time. Eara said, "Grams, you didn't give me my God blesses, yet."

At this point in their relationship, many times Eara would address Fran as "Grams" or "Mommy." Although Fran knew she wasn't replacing Andrea, it was a compliment to her to be called by those names. In addition at this point in time, it became obvious that grandparents do play an integral part in the lives of their grandchildren. In particular Fran and Jess loved this child as though she were their very own. Not only that, Eara also loved them, so!

Eara was becoming more and more conscious of styles by now and her habits were improving. She insisted upon her nightly bath. She put her hair up every night. She wanted clean clothes every morning. She began to take great pride in her manner of dressing. She didn't have to be told to use deodorant. She didn't have to be reminded to hang up her clothes. She was permitted to choose her clothes insofar as was practical. However, because of her weight problem, Eara came to realize she could not always wear the same styles a her friends wore. She had to get "plus" sizes and occasionally that brought about some disagreement as to what she would select and what Fran wanted her to buy. She did, however, like nice clothes and learned to coordinate them very well. Her "Grams" was very proud of her new attitudes about self, public appearances and instinctive worthiness.

Eara was now entering on the threshold of being eleven years old. Fran and others had set certain examples in Eara's life for her to follow. They set examples, which personified, that through the spirit of endearing LOVE, Conquering LOVE:

- Does not behave unseemly.
- Seeks nothing for one's own gratification.
- Is not easily provoked.
- Does not attempt to purposefully conjure up evil.
- Can triumph over all of life's adversities of: sickness, depression, disappointments, discontent, failures, dispirited feelings of self-worth, hostilities, jealousy, misbehavior and tragedy.

Four
When Love and Hope Interact

When LOVE and HOPE interact, LOVE hopes: sooner than later a transformation will occur; a change will move one from disorientation to re-orientation to new orientation; the inward grace will outshine and outreflect the outward disgrace. When LOVE and HOPE interact, LOVE builds up confidence, belief, faith, hope in all things and trust to triumph over all of life's adverse situations. Hope instills sufficient inward grace to give courage and strength to overcome all of life's negative impacts. When LOVE and HOPE interact LOVE and HOPE liberate by providing valuable additive resources to overcome life's obstacles.

To find LOVE and HOPE in such action, as stated above, let us see how Fran, along with Jess, moved Eara through continuing seasons of disorientation to re-orientation to new orientation, from pre-eleven years old to the threshold of becoming thirteen.

It was now about early April of 1983 and Todd sent a check for $1500.00, supposedly to repay all of the money he had been demanding to be sent back to him and which he received. As a matter of fact, by his requests and receipts, Todd practically broke Eara's savings account. If it were not for Eara's grandparents she would have become one more impecunious brat on the streets of Dayton. And, in this regard, before a month had passed, Todd called and asked for $500.00 of the money to be returned to him. This did not set well with Fran.

"Boy, what is the matter with you? I am not going to condone or proliferate this type of two-faced behavior any longer. I will not respond to your request. This is your daughter's savings plan for her future. Not yours!"

Todd angrily retorted, "Woman, if you don't shut your holier than thou trap and send me my money, pronto, you'll be sorry."

Fran just hung up the phone in total disgust.

However, this exchange of communication over Todd's monetary request was not over by a long shot. A further call came from a woman in New York at 2:30 A.M. one morning. This call greatly disturbed Jess and Fran, as Jess answered the phone.

"This better be a very, very, very close friend in need or an emergency. Who is it and what do you want at this hour in the morning?"

"Mister, if you care about our son, be advised, send him the money he asked for, within two hours, if not, he'll be dead meat!"

Jess hung up the phone and relayed the message to Fran. Fran became very frightened, not knowing whether someone was playing a prank or threatening Todd or just what was happening.

Fran and Jess could not go back to sleep until hours later worrying about what might be happening to Todd. Fran's response to the situation was to keep LOVE and HOPE alive and well. Her faith proved to be right, although the consequences were not what she expected.

Within a few days later, Todd surprisingly appeared at their house and demanded the money, all of it, the entire $1500.00 plus whatever other small amount that remained in Eara's savings account. In fact, he demanded all of the money he had been sending from time to time to Fran for deposits.

Fran and Jess became scared of the beast that was in their presence. They became even more scared as they peeped out of the window and then went to the door to get a closer look at the dark limousine waiting for Todd at the curb. They became terribly frightened and thought that Todd was maybe under duress of some New York drug kingpin and his hoodlums. So in a matter of thirty minutes or so the issue was resolved by Eara, Fran and Jess going to the National City Bank, followed by the gang and then withdrawing all of Eara's savings and handing it over to Todd. Todd took all of the money and began to leave without even saying, "Thank you and good bye."

Eara was so hurt and in tears, after witnessing such behavior from the father she worshipped so. So she had to say what was on her mind, being one accustomed to having the last word.

While they were still in the bank and with tears streaming down her cheeks, "Father, I am extremely disappointed in you. This has to be the lowest of the low moments you have brought into my life. Plus I was planning to use some of my savings to attend a summer camp in New York, this year. Now I have nothing and I will not be able to attend the summer camp! You are despicable!" Shaking her head, she added, "Dad, you are worse than a despicable human being, you are a gutter rat!"

Her words cut Todd to the bone. He finally relented and handed Eara $400.00 and kept on walking out of the bank without looking back. He crossed the street and got into the limousine and he and his bosom buddy took off in the opposite direction, from the bank, toward West Third Street in Dayton.

Jess, in a rare unchristian-like manner, wished Todd did look back, in hope that he would have walked into a glass door and badly harmed himself. Eara and Fran wondered why Jess looked to heaven and quietly said to himself, "Father forgive me."

Fran silently remained in shock concerning this entire, dramatic episode of vulgar human behavior that Todd injected into all of their lives, especially Eara's. After also being a witness of such mundane and monstrous behavior, Fran came to envision that Todd, who had been, at one time, such a loving and respectful son, had become a despicable stranger. Yet, inwardly, Fran still loved her son and hoped that one day he would change his life style and behavior, if not for himself, for his precious daughter's sake. The three of them returned home in utter dismay over Todd's behavior.

While still in town, Todd attempted to make further amends with Eara. However, his choice of doing so was just as bad as all of the other fatherly mistakes he had made so far. He decided to take Eara to see four movies in the same number of days. Todd played one of the characters in one of the movies. After questioning Eara and getting the word on this particular movie, from other adults, Fran felt this movie was too indecent for Eara to be seeing, due to the language.

To add insult to injury, it was also made known that Todd's bosom buddy, a young man, was a known drug addict and Todd had him chauffeuring the two of them (he and Eara) around town. One can only imagine the things Eara heard and saw while in the company of those two hoodlums.

This continuing saga of bad decision-making for and in the presence of his innocent, young daughter, irritated Fran so much so that she and Todd had another argument. When he dropped Eara off and came inside to say goodbye, Fran "lit" into him.

"Boy, if I've told you once, I've told you a thousand times, you are a hypocritical, no good, lying son of a gun. You are the worst example of an irresponsible, neglectful, poor decision-making father I've ever seen. You should be ridiculously ashamed of yourself after exposing your daughter to such a filthy movie and placing her in the company of thugs and drug addicts."

"Woman, you don't know what in the hell you are talking about. You are a seventy-five-year-old, holier than thou, trying to be a Christian, disgusting nag. You need to go and jump in a river somewhere. You are a piece of work!"

"And you are nothing but a wasted mass of protoplasm. There is no way you could have come from my loins. I spawned an ignoramus!"

On the last remark, Todd turned himself around and went out of the door and left town without saying goodbye.

Each and every time Todd and/or Andrea popped into their lives, Fran always sensed that trouble lay ahead for the three of them. It was like dealing with a dual losing tag team of wrestlers or a singular losing wrestler. Each and every time Andrea and/or Todd popped up, Fran always sensed she, Eara and Jess would have to step into life's gigantic boxing ring to deal with deceit, disappointment, disgrace, hidden agendas, jealousy, lying, profane attacks and/or ulterior motives. Each time Todd popped up, he brought havoc into Eara's young life. The same sentiment can be said of Andrea.

As a matter of fact, during the latter part of the summer of 1984, Andrea called Fran and asked if she could come and visit with Eara. Again putting LOVE and HOPE in action, of course, Fran consented. Andrea popped up after school closed and stayed at a very undesirable motel along German Town Pike, on the outer southwest suburb of Dayton. Fran and Jess wondered why she didn't stay with them, as she had from time to time. Immediately Fran sensed something was amiss. Andrea spent very little time with Eara and only came to visit with her, at the grandparents' home, after dark, each day. In fact she only spent three nights with Eara. During a happy moment, on the third night, Eara asked her mother a poignant question.

"Mother, would you please, please, please, take me home with you?"

"Baby girl, if I take you home with me, Grandma will have me arrested!"

"But why, mother?" By the look on her face, it was obvious to Andrea that Eara did not understand the legal ramifications that would occur if and when her mother just up and disappeared with her.

"Hopefully, one day, I'll be able to explain all of this mess I've introduced into your life."

Eara's teary-eyed request must have somehow touched Andrea's heart, for once in her life. So after the third night, Andrea shamefully crept out very early the next morning, before Eara awakened and went back to the motel. What was Andrea's ulterior motive for coming to visit with Eara? Creeping out so early in the morning left Eara in shock.

When Eara awoke and finding her mother not in bed beside her, she immediately ran to the kitchen, the common gathering place. Fran and Jess had already been up for at least two hours. They were now fixing breakfast.

"Gram, Grampa, have you seen my mother?"

Both replied with a look of disgust, "She crept out early, baby."

Consequently Eara, Fran nor Jess had any idea when she finally left town. It was later learned that she was pregnant and didn't want it to be detected. Why?

Where there is sadness LOVE and HOPE bring comfort. Where there is heart-brokenness LOVE and HOPE bring peace. Where there is emptiness LOVE and HOPE bring the fullness of joy and pleasures.

So for the balance of the summer, Eara was provided with a number of joyous activities and pleasures. She and her friend Nikki, again, went to camp for a week. And, again Eara immensely enjoyed the outing. Further, Nikki's mother and Fran made plans that allowed the two girls to attend several day camps. After the day camps closed, Eara spent several hours a day at the nearby Y.W.C.A. Eara had the opportunity to swim and play games with the other youngsters that were in attendance.

By September of 1984, Eara was nearly eleven years old and ready for the sixth grade of school. Everything went well until on October 17, 1984, on Eara's birthday, Andrea called Eara.

"Hey, baby girl, happy birthday!!! For once in my life I've also got some good news to tell you. And, I hope this will make you somewhat proud of your mother. I am now living in a brand spanking new apartment with three bedrooms, a large kitchen and dining area, and a large living room. More importantly this apartment has a big back yard with flower gardens along the edges."

"O, mother that sounds lovely. I hope to get to see it soon, one day."

"Well, that is why I called. Let me speak to Fran."

"Hey, Fran, I just told Eara that I am trying to turn my life around and I have a new apartment with all the trimmings of having an attached home with a beautiful back yard. So I'd like to have Eara come and live with us for good. Do you mind relinquishing custody of her?"

Fran became very nervous as the following thoughts rushed through her mind: Eara has so often expressed a desire to return to her mommy. If I insist on keeping them separated against Eara's will, Eara would probably rebel and perhaps dislike me forever. But this is not the time to let Eara go. So, after a few minutes of silent thoughts she finally responded:

"As I've always promised you, at such time when you become stabilized and responsible enough to keep Eara, I would have no objection of your request to keep Eara. However, at this time in her young life, I don't think we should be uprooting her while she is in the first term of the sixth grade of school."

With that response Andrea terminated any further conversation.

Sometime between her eleventh birthday and Christmas of 1984, the sum of Fran's thoughts and fears about Eara surfaced. Eara's lack of interest in school became more and more prevalent. Changes in her personality became noticeable. She lied more and more often about her homework. She would not bring her work home. Cooperation between her teachers and Fran academically brought little to no improvement. Eara just seemed to have lost interest.

Further, Eara's social standing and popularity in school was apparently of more interest than academics. She ran for Student Council that year and together she and Fran made posters and badges for her campaign, which she seemed to enjoy. By now she had become very popular and an interest in boys became apparent. Telephone calls during the evening interfered with her homework. Trying to alleviate her boredom and rapidly changing personality made parenting become more and more difficult for Fran and Jess.

In addition, respectively dealing with Todd's calls and his methods of trying to discipline Eara via the telephone and Andrea's calls trying to uplift Eara, these conditions were making Fran's responsibilities more and more difficult and complex.

Fran and Jess's lives were going through hell at this time just dealing with Eara's drastic change of behavior, lack of interest in academics and change of personality.

And, as if this were not enough for one to bear, not only dealing with Eara alone, but also Todd (via the long distance calls) and Fran began to disagree on certain issues. Coupled with this disagreement, Todd felt that Eara was too precious to be disciplined. There was no way Fran could not keep from becoming very frustrated in such a situation. To make matters worse for Fran, Eara was aware of the situation between mother and son. This was not good. To add insult to injury, Andrea called more often. And, although Andrea did not disagree, but rather encouraged discipline and even punishment if it were warranted, the frequency of her calls seemed to disturb Eara's feelings. In some instances Andrea's calls influence Eara's behavior patterns. What was the mother saying to her daughter? One can only imagine. This, too, added to Fran's frustration.

By now Eara was becoming more womanish than ever. The eleven-year-old girl had become a thirty-one-year-old. The eleven-year-old often put her grandmother on notice with arrogant and poignant reminders.

"You are not my mother! Perhaps, if you were, you would understand me better."

"You are not hip. Perhaps, if you were, you would realize it's not what you know, it is whom you know and that's how you get over. Social standing is more important than being a preppy nerd."

"In any event, you and grampa are not going to live forever. So I've got to listen, more often, to what dad and mother have to say, than what you two dictate to me."

With such reminders Fran and Jess often lost it.

But, to bring some semblance of peace, joy and happiness back into their lives, Fran and Jess had to search deep within themselves to keep one or the other from going to court for killing this child they so love. At this juncture in their lives, Fran and Jess, each had to get down to their "nefesh" to bring forth unending LOVE and HOPE.

As a matter of fact, under the current conditions and circumstances that were prevailing in her and Jess's home, Fran came to herself and fully realized that:

- So long as Eara was in she and Jess's home, she would have to deal with the father's hostility and jealousy.
- Andrea now wanted Eara more than ever to live with her (probably as the in-house baby sitter, etc.).
- If she kept Eara against her will, Eara would probably continue to rebel and perhaps become even more a problem child than she presently was.
- Eara knew the promise "Grams" made (to Andrea and/or Todd, that if either one of them ever became established with a decent home and capable

of parenting as a parent should) that she would relinquish custody of her so that she could go to live with whichever one became established first.
- Something had to be done.

Yet, at this point in time Fran naturally came to the decision that some changes had to be made.

As fate would have it, later in 1984, the family learned that Todd had landed a part in a television series and again he had to travel to California to make it. So Fran and Todd "buried the hatchet" and Todd started calling again, regularly. In November, either just before or shortly after Thanksgiving, Todd called once more.

"Hey, big momma, do you mind if Eara would spend her Christmas vacation with me?"

Though reluctant to give consent, Fran responded, "I don't see any harm in letting her do so. Maybe a change of location would be good for Eara's experience."

Though she had some apprehension about Eara going off into the wild blue yonder in California, Fran once again allowed LOVE and HOPE to take over. Fran thought perhaps, letting Eara experience this new environment, some, if not all, of Eara's pent-up arrogance, emotional instabilities, lack of interest in academics and longing to be away from her grandparents for a while, will all vanish.

In addition, having a sister-in-law in California whom she could trust and with whom Todd had visited a number of times, Fran hoped all would go well during this episode of Eara's young life. Plus, Eara was so excited and really wanted to go, as she wanted to see the California about which she had heard so much.

Todd, therefore, said that a prepaid ticket would be waiting at the Dayton Cox's Airport for Eara and that he would meet her when she arrived in California. Eara was to leave on the Sunday before Christmas 1984 and return home the following Thursday.

When Fran and Jess took Eara to the airport, there was no ticket for the trip. After some discussion, they decided to let Eara take the trip because her facial expressions indicated she was very disappointed. Eara's facial expressions showed she was very distraught over the thought of not getting to see California. So Fran and Jess (being the ever faithful and loving grandparents that they have been since this child was an infant) paid for the ticket and saw to it that Eara safely boarded the plane. They even waited to see if they could see where she sat on the plane, hoping to lovingly wave goodbye to her.

Immediately upon returning home, Fran called Ruth Ames, the sister-in-law. She explained to Ruth what had happened at the airport and asked her to meet Eara just in case big mouth, lying lips, ever-neglectful Todd failed to show up. Arrangements were made that if anything negative happened, Ruth was to return Eara to the grandparents on the next plane.

Yet, Fran's ever hopeful and loving heart, mind and soul had come full circle in regard to her feelings about her son. Fran thought that Todd could have possibly been delayed because of work or for some other reason. Strangely enough, even though Todd had previously disappointed Fran a number of times, somehow this time she believed his intentions were good.

As fate would have it, Todd was at the airport to meet Eara and they all went to Ruth's home. Ruth was a tall slender woman, who had married Jess' brother Raymond (now deceased). She loved to exercise and her sixty-five-year-old face and body appeared more like that of a forty-three-year-old woman. She also loved to cook and entertain guests. So Todd and Eara were gladly welcome into her home.

When Fran called at 4 P.M., Dayton, Ohio time, in the afternoon of Christmas Day 1984, Eara, Ruth and the family had just awakened and it was reported that:

- Early in the evening, on the Sunday before Christmas, Todd left Eara with Ruth and family and did not return until the next evening. No one knew where he was or what had happened to him.
- When he did appear, he told them that he had been involved in an accident and had been put into jail.

Nonetheless, Fran overlooked this report. Since she and Todd were now somewhat on peaceful terms and cordially agreeing and/or disagreeing agreeably. Fran also gave permission for Eara to stay with her father, per his request, until the Saturday following Christmas of 1984 instead of the Thursday following Christmas as originally planned.

As it happened, Todd put Eara on a plane at 12:45 A.M. Sunday morning, California time, and Eara had to change planes in St. Louis, Missouri. In the follow-up story, although Todd said he dispatched Eara to Dayton under the austere care of the airlines, Eara said that when she arrived in St. Louis, the stewardess went on her way. This was an awful thing to do to an eleven-year-child, even though she may have acted all grown up.

As fate, LOVE and HOPE controlled the circumstances, it just so happened that a couple from Dayton who had gone to California on the same plane as Eara, this couple was returning on the same flight as Eara. The couple lovingly led Eara the proper gate so that she was able to safely arrive home to her grandparents. Fran and Jess were graciously thankful.

When Fran and Jess met Eara, at the airport luggage area, to them, Eara appeared very exhausted to the point of being ill. After they arrived home, they allowed her to go to bed and rest for a little while. Having somewhat recuperated from her exhaustive trip, Fran, being the inquisitive one of the two (that is between she and Jess), asked Eara about her trip. Eara reported:

"While I was there, on the first day I arrived, father and I moved from his hotel to an apartment. His new apartment had no furniture. The first night, I had to sleep on a big rug on the floor. The following day he bought a blowup air mattress. That was a little more comfortable to sleep on. Also I met dad's friend from New York, a woman by the name of Heather Graham. She spent several days with us. She seemed like a nice person and we bonded very well. Most of the day on Christmas Eve, we spent a lot of time shopping and later trimming the Christmas tree."

After quietly listening to Eara's report of her trip (and, although, Fran was not pleased with some parts of the report) she finally responded to Eara by saying:

"Well, baby girl, considering all things being equal, it sounds like you enjoyed yourself and you are happy that you got to see some of the bustling life style of Californians. Let's go get something to eat."

On that note the two of them went into the living room and informed Jess of the dining out plans and the three of them went to "The Cracker Barrel" for dinner.

By now Eara had truly become an eleven-year-old going on thirty-one. She was adjusting well to her dad's emotional roller coaster way of life. She was becoming accustomed to hearing about her mother' pseudo new orientation to being a caring, loving, and responsible mother. She was very tolerant when hearing of the ongoing antagonism between her father and mother. So, as Eara's life saga continued, often Eara was not really sure which way to turn in the flux. At this point in her life, did she really want to spend the rest of her life with her dad, her grandparents or her mother? Only time will reveal the ultimate outcome.

Nonetheless, in the present context, while Todd secretly wanted custody of Eara, so did Andrea. And, as soon as Eara had returned home from California, Andrea continued to frequently call Fran, asking for custody of Eara to be returned to her. She reported to Fran:

"I am doing well and I feel I am capable of taking care of her."

Fran then in turn often asked Eara, "Do you want to go to live with your mother?"

Eara always responded with an affirmative, "Yes."

Todd was not pleased when he had heard from Fran concerning the pressurized attempted custody takeover.

He emphatically told Fran, "I would not go along with such a decision and more importantly I would fight for custody of Eara. As a matter of fact, I have already applied for a divorce and requested custody."

Fran in turn convincingly said to him several times, "You do not need the responsibility of a girl child."

However, during the conversation, several times Todd quickly and threateningly retorted, "I am not giving up on my request for custody. As a matter of fact, if I have to, I will abduct Eara. If necessary I will take her with me to California. And, there would be nothing you or Andrea could do about it!"

After going through the above mess, to bring some semblance of peace and harmony back into Eara's, Fran's and Jess' lives, Fran had to go deep to call on the indwelling spirit to give the strength and courage to put LOVE and HOPE in action once again and forever.

Fran surely needed such strength and courage because, in early 1985, Andrea's lawyer filed a motion for custody of Eara, with a court hearing set for August of the same year. In the petition it was mainly stated that:

- Andrea's condition and circumstances were now stabilized.
- Andrea believes it is best (that is in the best interest of the child) for Eara to be with her.
- Andrea now has a suitable home for her.

The petition also stated several other minor reasons supporting Andrea's case for having custody of Eara.

This legal battle between Fran, Andrea and Andrea' lawyer had become very cumbersome, depressing and exhaustive for Fran. Therefore Fran needed reasonable and worthy help to expedite the matter. Fran contacted Todd in an effort to convince him that (due to his changing life style and frequent change of residence, et al.; since Eara especially wanted to live with her mother; since he was still living in the same deplorable neighborhood; since he had no housekeeper; she didn't feel that Eara needed to be with him) the custody of Eara should be given to Andrea.

Todd, still in disagreement with this legal action, emphatically responded, "When the school is in the final session before closing for its summer recess, I'll be there to get her!"

After listening to Todd's response, Fran just hung up

the phone. She enlisted some discussion with Jess. Then she silently went to her room to ponder more on the situation, since no final action had been determined by the Court at this point in time.

In the midst of the ongoing legal battle, Fran remembered that Jethro, Andrea's father, told her in the late summer of 1974 that Andrea was pregnant with a second child. So, with all of this on her mind, Fran:

- Was trying to decide what's best for Eara.
- Felt that perhaps with Andrea being older and wiser, she should be more capable of mothering.
- Was finding that the situation was becoming more and more difficult to undertake.
- Came to realize, it appeared that nothing she did was appreciated or was enough.
- Also came to realize, although she was certain that she knew what was best for Eara, she wanted to do what was best for all concerned.

Yet while Fran was still pondering on the legal battles concerning Eara, the end of the 1984–1985 school year was fast approaching. To unknowingly add more drama to Fran's worries, Eara had invited both of her parents to attend her sixth grade recognition day.

And, in the meantime, Eara had not been told of her mother's pregnancy with a second child. Fran really didn't expect either of them to come because the mother came so seldom and the father had disappointed the child so often. Fran was very much in doubt that either of them would be there. On the contrary, on the morning of recognition day several uncomfortable actions occurred.

First, just as Eara was to leave home for school, the

school called asking to speak to Todd. The caller stated that Todd had called and they had given him the wrong time that the Programme would be held. Obviously he did not leave a call back number for them to reach him and not having heard from him in a while, nor knowing how to contact him, he could not be notified of the change. Although he did not get to attend the Programme, he had arrived in town.

Second, Andrea called, stating that she and her father had arrived and asked for directions to the school. Eara was ecstatic that morning when Fran told her that her mother had arrived. Fran met Andrea and her father and the new baby at the school. At the time of the meeting, Andrea appeared ashamed for Fran to see that she had a second child. Why? On the contrary, Eara was very happy to see her mother and accepted the baby as though she was not surprised. The other local members of the family did not know about the second child until Andrea's and her father's appearance.

Following the Programme, Fran told Eara not to take the school bus home, but to wait for her to pick her up. Fran was aware and afraid that Todd would attempt to abduct Eara as he threatened to do so.

After giving Eara her instructions, Fran, Jess, Andrea and baby, Jethro and a few other close family members had lunch at a nearby Red Lobster Restaurant. While there the family ran into the local attorney, Shirley Burger, whom Fran had procured to handle Andrea's custody case. (The legal action had to be initiated by a local attorney for Andrea to regain custody of Eara.) After meeting the local attorney, Jethro later informed Fran that Andrea had also retained a lawyer in her hometown, Troy, New York, just in case Andrea would run into difficulty in Ohio.

While the families were in reunion, simultaneously the illegal war or fracas had begun at the school. Following lunch, later on just as Fran and Jess were leaving home to go to the school to get Eara, the principal called stating that Todd was there. He reported Todd had been giving them a hard time because he wanted to get his child. He had a limousine waiting and was very adamant because the principal was following orders in not allowing anyone but her grandparents to pick Eara up. Without a shadow of a doubt, Fran was convinced, Todd was there to abduct Eara in order to keep Andrea from taking her away.

Fran and Jess both instructed the principal to hold out and hold on, and to call the local police if necessary, until they arrived. Once they arrived they ignored Todd, quickly secured Eara in their company, got into the car and posthaste left the school premises.

Todd followed them for a few steps toward the car and literally cursed obscenities, then finally left the school premises to seek temporary residence in the city until this legal war was over.

In the meantime, local attorney Shirley Burger called the grandparents' home. Inasmuch a the court in Ohio granted custody to Fran, it was also necessary for an attorney in the same city to take action to terminate the custody. So, upon returning the attorney's call, Attorney Burger informed Fran that she had drawn up an Agreement granting custody of Eara to Andrea. She added, that if it were possible to get Todd to sign it, while in town, the case would be finalized and no court hearing would be necessary. In addition, this would eliminate the necessity of Andrea and Todd having to return in August.

So, in the meantime, Todd was contacted to be at his parents' home around 5:30 P.M. The main thought was to facilitate the expediency of this legal action. About 5:30 P.M. the attorney brought the Agreement to Fran and Jess' home after she closed her office. As usual, Fran (in an attempt to once again keep LOVE and HOPE alive) really felt that Todd would sign the agreement. She felt Todd would sign the agreement especially after he talked with Eara who had emphatically said to him that she wanted to go with mother. Obviously Fran's feelings were not conjured up in Todd's heart, mind and soul.

When confronted with it, Todd insisted that Andrea was unfit to have the child and refused to sign the Agreement. Attorney Burger then stated that if Fran agreed to allow Eara to go with Andrea for an extended visit, Todd could take the Custody Agreement, which she had drawn up, to his lawyer for his scrutiny and then return it to her by mail. Todd disagreeably agreed and accepted the latter proposal and all went their separate ways.

Andrea planned to leave on the following day, so Jethro, she and baby went to a motel to spend the night.

Before bedtime, Fran told Eara that she could not go to school the next day (which was the last day of school) for fear that Todd would carry out his threats and abduct her. This instruction did not go over well with Eara. She threw a tantrum, fell down on the floor and threatened to kill herself. Upset by Eara's actions, Fran called Andrea at the motel and asked her to come and talk to Eara.

Sensing the problems that were confronting Eara and fearing Todd's actions, Fran finally relented and sent Eara home with Andrea, and cautioned them to get out of town as early as they can.

The following day, Todd called and threatened to have Fran arrested for violating the court order. Fran did not hear from Todd any more for sometime. On Jess's behalf and her own, Fran had had enough of the whole mess. It really was time to let go and let God. It was time to truly exemplify LOVE and HOPE in action.

Within six months after Eara went to live with her mother, she began to regurgitate some of the same old problems. She didn't like school and wasn't doing well academically. However, she and Fran spoke often by phone. During one of their first conversations, Eara told Fran that, "Mommy bought me a pair of drop earrings and a mini skirt. Mommy also lets me hang out at the mall. Mommy allows me to stay up late and watch cable television. Mommy has had another child."

Upon hearing this conversation, the only response Fran could muster up was, "Baby girl, please don't let all of this lackadaisical spirit, levity and newfound pseudo freedom get the best of you. Do you understand me?"

With Fran having the last word, they hung up the phones. However, within a few weeks later, when Eara sent a photograph, Fran could envision from the photo, that Eara was maturing much too fast for a pre-twelve-year-old.

Now that Eara is with her mother, Fran often looks in retrospect and ruminates over the growth and development of her precious granddaughter. The hurt experienced with her being gone was like nothing Fran had ever experienced before. In fact, she:

- Lost interest in most things.
- Lost the desire to go out.
- Just seemed not to be able to adjust to Eara's absence.
- Would suddenly burst out in tears, and actually for a while,
- Feared that she would have a nervous breakdown.

- Attended church regularly, but hated to go.

She hated to go to church because of so many friends asking about Eara, and she couldn't talk about her without crying. Further, when the junior choir sang, she cried. When attending a program where tapes were shown with Eara playing her flute, she cried. The loss was overwhelming.

Yes Fran cried for days, for weeks, for months. Yet in her tears of sorrow, Fran exemplified the essence of LOVE and HOPE in action. At this juncture in Eara's life, Fran continued to exemplify the kind of LOVE and HOPE that provides courage and strength to overcome the pain of:

- Deceptive giving and vulgar human behavior.
- Exposing a youngster to the gutter-most and trashiest attribute in human life.
- Heartbreak brought on by disappointing parental behavior.
- Depression and loss of interest in the value additive things in life.
- Low self-esteem and low self-worth.
- Arrogant and rude poignant behavior.
- The ugliness of custodial battles.
- Parental arguments, disagreements and other domestic adversity.
- Accepting it is time for a change.
- Of losing a loved one to another less caring, compassionate, lovable, and qualified individual.

Five
When Love Believes and Provides

WHEN LOVE BELIEVES AND PROVIDES, LOVE sacrificially gives all and does all for one and all at no charge. WHEN LOVE BELIEVES AND PROVIDES, LOVE is compassionate and dedicates, is kind and protects, and is not self-seeking but always believes, hopes, perseveres and trusts. WHEN LOVE BELIEVES AND PROVIDES, LOVE bestows not only material comforts but also the full essence of spiritual fruit. WHEN LOVE BELIEVES AND PROVIDES, LOVE bestows the kind of spiritual fruit that helps one and all to get beyond all of our yesterdays, today, and tomorrows.

Eara was in that very crucial and critical period of her life wherein she had to move through Junior High School to High School experiences to new life style experiences outside of the academic setting(s), from age 13–17.

Let us see how Fran by and through LOVE AND BELIEF in Eara, along with the hidden assistance of Jess, persevered and attempted again and again and again to provide not only material comforts but also spiritual joys for Eara.

In the fall, prior to the beginning of the Junior High School year, Fran shopped, sent and provided enough school supplies to last for several months of the year.

And, now that Eara was living with her mother and

her little sisters, Fran called Eara every week for a while. Many times Eara, in conversation, said that she was baby-sitting her little sisters, while Andrea was out allegedly having a fling and/or working. Although, Eara seemed discontented, each time Fran asked her if she wanted to come back to live with she and Jess, Eara's answer was the same, an emphatic "No." This response was a great surprise to Fran, as she was attempting to provide some comfort of sanity into the mind-set of her precious granddaughter, whom she loved dearly.

Also while in her season of seemingly discontentment, Fran even tried to provide some joy and peace for Eara by contacting the Social Agency in the area, in which Andrea and the three children lived. This idea was conjured up in Fran's mind upon hearing of the new baby in the home. Therefore, she called the Social Agency and asked that the home be investigated for fitness of the mother. The Social Agency representative reported that the home and mother received a favorable grade. Thus Fran decided to give up having Andrea et al. investigated for a while.

Not only did Eara seem discontented but also it seemed strange to Fran that Eara was always in need of something. So for her birthday on October 17, 1986, Fran shopped and provided several beautiful dresses, slacks, etc. for Eara. In this context, it was reported that Andrea was wearing some of Eara's clothing and was not properly taking care of them.

As if the latter was not doing enough for Eara, at Christmas time Fran bought and provided more clothes for Eara, as well as toys for the two smaller children. In addition Fran always provided and sent a huge box containing fruit, candy, and other Christmas gifts.

Similarly, Fran provided and sent clothes for Easter

and then for summer of 1987. Fran practically provided and dressed Eara until she grew to the point where she wanted to select her own clothes. And, because Eara wanted to select her own clothes rather than to continue wearing the outdated choice of clothing Fran was sending her, Fran then opted to start sending money to Eara, so that Eara can purchase her own choice of clothes, etc.

In fact, further on down the road, Fran began to send gift certificates. On one occasion, Andrea informed Fran that it might not be a good idea to keep sending gift certificates for Eara since Eara carelessly lost a $50.00 certificate. However, it was never really and truthfully explained what happened to that gift certificate. Did Eara lose it or did Andrea use Eara's money for herself?

Apparently as time elapsed, Eara had greater issues to deal with than having and/or losing money. By the time she was 13 going on 33, Andrea had to take her to a counselor. She just could not seem to adjust. Eara's transformation of character, coupled with specific mood swings, presented nightmares for Andrea. However, as Fran noted, Andrea didn't call her until she realized that she just could not handle the problems and headaches, which Eara was currently displaying before her mother. During this period of Eara's young life, Todd had not seen her for some time and perhaps had no idea of what his precious daughter was going through.

To complicate Eara's life more than it already was, Andrea enrolled Eara into one school and then another. To help in alleviating this juggling of schools for Eara, Fran respectively suggested to Andrea and Todd to send Eara to a private school. Neither parent would entertain or agree to such a suggestion, even though once again Fran offered to pay the tuition. This decline on the part of the parents showed that even when providential blessings are lovingly provided, they are often despised and rejected by fools.

Since Eara's parents could not or did not want to be motivated to move Eara out of a context of disorientation to re-orientation to a place that provided new orientation for growth of self-worth and well-being, in Fran's estimation, by adolescence, Eara was living like a dysfunctional 18-year-old. Further, Andrea informed Fran that the Junior High School, which Eara attended, was connected to the High School by a walk through. Consequently, many times when Eara should have been in class she was over in the High School gym watching the older boys play basketball.

This issue did not sit well with Fran. Therefore, she called the Junior High School's principal's office in an attempt to arrest Eara's newly developed wayward behavior. However, the bottom line response to the problem was that Eara was frequently missing school due to taking care of her younger sisters.

Eara's newly developed wayward behavior brought on fearful dimensions for Andrea and Fran. One morning at 1:30 A.M. Andrea called Fran upset and in fear that her child was perhaps kidnapped and/or raped and/or killed.

"Fran, it's 1:30 in the morning and I don't know where that child of mine is at this time in the morning. She has not come home from a basketball game. No Junior High or High School basketball team is playing at this hour in the morning. Where could she be? I don't know what to do."

Fran frantically responded, "Andrea, listen to me, get a next door neighbor you can trust to baby sit, call the police office and report your child is missing and let whoever answers know you are on your way there. Call me back as soon as you cannnn."

Before they could hang up, as Andrea was looking out of the living room window, she could see Eara walking alone, down the street on which they lived.

Fran continued talking, "Is she hurt? Is she safe? Why is she out on the streets this hour in the morning?"

Andrea, in a hurry to get to Eara, cut the conversation short and said to Fran, "I have no answers to your questions, but this heifer will have some answers to mine. Bye."

Missing classes and out late attending basketball games were not the only problems Andrea and Eara had to deal with at this time.

According to Jethro in an updated report to Fran, Andrea was working at night and leaving Eara with the two little ones, doing as she wished. In addition, he intimated that Andrea was on drugs and often slept so sound that she didn't know what was going on in Eara's room.

When Fran heard this report as usual she became livid and almost lost it. In her forgiving spirit and looking at the situation in the greater light, her heart and mind wondered what could she provide to lift Eara out of such a chaotic and demeaning mess.

So, she relayed all of the alleged information to Todd. In Fran's estimation, apparently Todd was not able to squarely face or tackle the situation, because in his usual manner, Todd did nothing nor did he respond to anyone.

Hence having been reminded by the Court that Eara was still her responsibility, even though she was living with her mother, Fran requested that Andrea's (temporary) custody be terminated. Fran's primary reason for the request was based on the report of so many negatives that Andrea and Eara were doing.

So, to get Eara as soon as she possibly could out of her chaotic and demeaning mess, Fran was again thinking how could she provide a more conducive environment for Eara to change direction in her present life style. In November of 1987, either some time before or just after Thanksgiving, Fran called Todd and asked him to bring Eara to spend Christmas with her grandparents. Acting on Todd's promise to bring Eara home to Dayton, Fran, Jess, et al. planned all of the holiday festivities to focus on the whim of Eara and Todd. A day or so before Christmas Eve, Fran called Todd.

"Hey, son, what time will you and my precious one be arriving in Dayton?"

"We are going to stop in New York City. So I am letting Eara spend a short time with her Aunt Lee and cousins as she expressed her desire to see them. Other than that I cannot say for sure when we are going to arrive in Dayton."

Providential LOVE always believes, hopes, and trusts in a promise. But, this promise was by lying lips, full of excuses, disappointing Todd. Christmas Eve and Christmas Day, 1985 passed, no Todd, no Eara. After three days passed, Fran called one of the cousin's home.

"Todd did not say anything to us about going to Dayton. As a matter of fact he and Eara ate Christmas dinner with us. And, as usual, after getting his belly full, he left Eara with us and Todd lit out of here like a man on a mission. We have not heard from him or have any idea where he could be, since his bumblebee departure. However, he has called daily and promised to pick Eara up and that was three days ago."

"Thank you for the information. Let me speak to Lee, please." After handing Lee the phone, Fran continued.

"Tell me in secret, so Eara cannot hear you, how is

the child's outward appearance? How does she look physically? Does she have two or three suitcases full of clothes and shoes?"

"Girl, no. She looks somewhat sickly to me. And, as for the clothes she is wearing, they look like dirt rags. They are the only clothes she has with her. She sleeps and gets up in the same clothes. And, the one pair of shoes she had were so badly worn, she had put some cardboard in the bottom to keep her feet from getting wet or injured if it rained or if she accidentally walked on some broken glass or pebbles. But don't worry about her feet. My George bought her a new pair of boots."

"After listening to all that you have reported, Lee, please, please, please do a big favor for me. Take Eara back home to Andrea."

"I hear your plea. But to tell you the truth, Eara needed to be away from her mother, her sisters, that place Andrea calls home and that environment in which she has been living and haphazardly going to school, for the past 12 months or so. I would not suggest returning her to such depressing circumstances at this time."

"Girl, you have said a mouthful. Let's leave her where she is!"

They hung up the phones and Fran went into the living room to bring Jess up-to-date concerning the health, welfare and whereabouts of his precious granddaughter.

Inasmuch as Fran wanted to provide a comfortable place and environment for her granddaughter to rest, recuperate and regroup, the only thing she could do is hope, be patient, and wait.

Faithfully waiting paid off. On New Year's Day 1987, at approximately 4:30 A.M., the doorbell rang and upon answering, Todd and Eara were standing there. Naturally, Mr. Loose Lips opened up his mouth and without a proper greeting began right away with his plethora of lies and excuses. He told Fran and Jess that they had taken a plane from New York to Cleveland, Ohio and had come from Cleveland by way of a van to Dayton.

Fran and Jess immediately recognized Todd's line of false, slick talk. They looked at each other and simultaneously said, "Let's move on." To each of them Eara appeared extremely tired. They suggested a bath for her and to go to bed. In the meantime Todd told of the several beautiful dresses he had purchased for Eara.

The following day Todd took Eara shopping and bought many gifts for her. They spent most of the day shopping and when they returned home, Todd called one of Eara's friends and asked if she would like for Eara to spend the night with her. Eara spent the night with her friend and Todd spent the night with his "in town" buddies.

Fran was so hurt to think that with only a few hours to spend, he took Eara away and planned for the two of them to be away from her grandparents. He knew the following day was a Sunday and that they had to leave in order for Eara to be back in school on Monday.

All that Fran, Jess and the family had planned and provided was a waste of their precious time and money. Why would such a monster do such a painful thing to his compassionate, kind, and loving parents?

Fran had rudely come to the realization that, although it had taken a number of years to accept the fact, it was true without a doubt that Todd was jealous of the love, which existed between Eara and her grandparents and would do anything to hurt his mother. Yes, it was obvious and had been shown many times, but Fran, being a Christian and wanting to do the right thing by and for the child, just didn't want to believe it.

After Eara had returned to Troy, New York and to school, any semblance of academic improvement went from bad to worse. Andrea reported to Fran, although she again enrolled Eara in different schools:

- Nothing changed.
- Her schoolwork did not improve at all.
- She had to repeat the 8th grade.
- She returned to the Junior High for 9th grade. She failed that also.

Fran believed that part of this ongoing academic failure was:

- Largely due to the fact that Eara had too many absences caused by her having to stay at home to be the babysitter for the younger children.
- Attributed to the same problems—cutting classes, skipping school and hanging out with the wrong crowd.

Fran's strong belief in her granddaughter that Eara can do better than what appears on the surface, propelled Fran to investigate other academic avenues which she could afford to provide so that Eara can move out of her academic failure mode.

First, Fran contacted the school and talked with the assistant principal. He advised her that they had referred Eara to a Probate Court counselor. Why? The Counselor reported, a number of times, to Fran that:

- Eara had the ability to learn but just didn't have the interest and would not attend school regularly.

- Her mother is to blame for Eara's problems.

Second, in the meantime, Fran wrote and requested applications from a private school in Richmond, Indiana. The school's Admission's Office was willing to accept Eara's application. It was a school for emotionally disturbed children. The school was approximately 30 miles, west of Dayton, Ohio. Thus, the grandparents could easily visit and keep tabs on Eara's progress. Fran offered to pay the tuition. But, both parents refused to let Eara move out of her environment of disorientation and to attend this special school.

Third, Fran then contacted a school in Piney Woods, Mississippi where the student could work and help pay for his/her own tuition. The school had been highly recommended by a friend of the family who had sent her daughter there and was well satisfied with the results. More importantly, this school had a well-structured program, a band, a choral group, and offered many interesting activities, and the students were obligated to attend church on Sunday. Within this context, again, Fran sent all the necessary application forms for Andrea to fill out. Again, Andrea refused to let Eara attend such a school.

As fate would have it, when fools turn down providential love and caring because they want to be the little gods in control, the inevitable happens.

One night, in the midst of being sick and tired of her way of life, of being abused and misused, of being depressed and oppressed, Eara called Fran.

"Grams, I am very unhappy with my life. I am equally unhappy with mother. We are having problems! Could I come back and live with you and Grampa Jess?"

"God bless you, baby. That would be fine. However, you'll have to attend private school for a year."

"Grams, mother told me that you would make that a prerequisite for returning to live with you and grampa. I don't want to do that. If I have to do that, I'd rather stay here."

On that response they hung up the phones and Fran had realized the devil in Andrea used the latter statement about going to private school, as a weapon, indicating that Fran did not really want her to come back home to Dayton.

Eara was now fifteen years old and she ran away from home and stayed with one of the family friends. **She and her friend obtained part-time jobs.** More importantly, when Andrea discovered where Eara was staying, she acquired police assistance and brought Eara back to her home. However, Eara, always the one to have the last word, told the police that she didn't want to live with her mother and sisters ever again. On that note the police referred her to Probate Court. When Fran was informed of these latest episodes in Eara's life, she contacted the Probate Court with intentions of returning Eara to Ohio. However (miss now more than womanish than ever before), Eara maintained that she did not want to come back.

Although the court in Troy gave Fran permission to regain custody of Eara, after talking with her attorney and taking everything into consideration (five years having passed, Eara's age, and the fact that she didn't want to come back), Fran decided that it was better that Eara didn't come back, lest she would rebel and Fran would not be able to handle her.

During this stage of growing out of silent frustration and silent turmoil in Eara's life, Todd was now in California looking for work. Andrea was working at a better paying job and was able to provide and place Eara in a boarding school.

Eara had learned many things while in this school, and though Fran was not able to visit the school, pictures of it portrayed that it was a beautiful setting up in the hills of upper New York, and Eara seemed to like it very much.

Eara was now "coming to herself" on a daily basis. So, Fran was happy to call and talk with her often on a more pleasant basis. Now, at least it was such a joy for Fran to hear Eara say at the end of each call, "Grams, I love you." Fran even felt that Eara seemed to be growing up somewhat.

Yes, Fran felt a bit of animosity toward Andrea for having gone to court about Eara, but Fran knew that it was the best thing for Eara. In fact, Fran shudders when she thinks of what could have happened had Eara worked long enough to save money enough to get to New York City or somewhere else, and had been lost along with the thousands of runaways, which everyone and everywhere so often reads and hears about.

Meanwhile Todd didn't contact the family anymore until the latter part of February 1990, at which time he called from Cincinnati, Ohio about 50–55 miles south of Dayton, Ohio. His call was to inform Fran and Jess that he had a part in a play at one of the theatres. In fact, his call was quite a surprise after not having heard from him for months.

He came to spend the night and Fran was so happy to see that he looked so much better and seemed happy to be home. He said the show would be running for approximately five weeks. In Fran's estimation, Todd even appeared to be feeling much better. This made Fran very happy, of course.

Eara came home to spend the weekend, during the third week of the show, as Todd was visiting with the family. On this happy occasion all of them went to the performance, along with Fran's two sisters, and they had a very delightful evening. Todd's performance was great and he got a standing ovation. All being on one accord, Eara, Fran, Fran's sisters, Jess and Todd had dinner out after the show. After dinner, Eara spent the night with her grandparents. They tremendously enjoyed her. She and "Grams" talked about her school activities, the parties she attended, her boy friends, and other typical teenage things. By now Eara had developed into a very attractive young lady. Each time Fran saw Eara, she loved her more, and each time their parting was more difficult.

During his stay in Cincinnati, Todd was suffering quite a bit with an arthritic knee. However, no one could detect his ailment by the way he performed. After the show closed, he spent three weeks in clubs in the Dayton area. Fran was very glad at this time because from all indications, Todd no longer appeared to be drinking any appreciable amount of alcohol. And, before returning to New York, he expressed a desire to move back to Dayton. He even expressed his hopes of bringing Eara home and perhaps that they would share whatever dwelling he was able to afford. However, after leaving town, Fran heard no more from him for about a month.

On this accord, as Fran continued her silent expressions and exemplifications of WHEN LOVE BELIEVES AND PROVIDES, it appeared that fate could change people's feelings and thoughts. For Eara, this was a shining example of LOVE expressed at its highest level.

From this point, the grandparents visibly saw a new

Eara as the months flew by. Eara called several times and near the summer she became very excited because her boyfriend had invited her to attend his senior prom as his date. The school had also acted in her interest and had given her permission to attend the prom. Fran had provided her money to buy a new formal and Fran was nearly as excited as Eara was about her attending the prom. The following week, his family invited her to the parents' home to be his guest at his graduation. This also made Eara very happy.

So excited that she had the opportunity to attend a prom, after the gala event, Eara sent pictures of her and her boyfriend, and one of her alone in her formal dress. Fran was equally overjoyed and thought Eara looked beautiful—the picture of health.

Nevertheless, as there are life events that bring joy, there are also life events that bring sadness and worry. In early July of 1990, Andrea called all worried and upset thinking that she was going to lose her first born.

"Fran where have you been? I've been trying to reach you all day. I am here at the hospital where Eara has undergone emergency surgery. The doctor had to put a fistula into her arm so that she could go on kidney dialysis. Each of Eara's kidneys was only functioning at 25 percent."

"You are where? What is happening to my baby girl? Tell me again, slowly this time." Andrea repeated the facts. In shock and surprised, Fran retorted.

"Why did you wait until now to tell me Eara had a health problem? After all, it has only been a few months ago that she was with us and at that time she seemed perfectly healthy to me, us!"

"I am sorry, I've been dealing with my own problems on this end. More importantly, Eara has been under the care of an urologist for the past three months. The deterioration of her kidneys has been occurring very rapidly. It was the school physician who discovered Eara's condition during a routine physical checkup. I'll keep you abreast if any serious changes in her condition occur. Let me get back to my baby. Bye."

With Andrea having her hands full, trying to keep up with her job, hospital visitations, two other little ones to care for, the upkeep of her apartment, bills, maintenance on her car, etc. she just did not have the time to call Fran as often as she would have otherwise done so.

So in August, the grandparents still agonizing over Eara's situation and not being able to stand it any longer, they journeyed to New York to see Eara. But why did they wait so long to do so?

There was quite a change in her appearance. Her eyes showed tiredness. Her complexion was sallow and she wasn't her usual exuberant self. The day after Fran and Jess arrived, Eara had an appointment at the hospital for X-rays, ultrasound, and blood tests, in order to try and determine why such rapid deterioration of her kidneys. The following week her dialysis treatments started, two times a week, three hours each time. However, according to Andrea, for some unknown reason, hospital personnel said the tests were not completed due to her kidneys being small or some such reason.

As Eara was going through this season of sickness and doubt as to whether she was going to make it or not, she was very thankful to her grandparents for their presence. Just having them present provided joy, hope and a resurgent belief that through God all things are possible. By their presence, she knew then that God provides, through God's miraculous love, the inner strength and belief to overcome her present kidney failure condition.

As time elapsed and as Fran and Jess observed Eara slowly recovering and as they realized there was nothing else they could do, they returned to Dayton. Once home, Fran kept close contact with Eara by calling every two or three days, to ask how she was feeling, since Eara was now undergoing dialysis three times a week for four hours each time. Fran would say to her. "Hi baby, this is your guardian angel. How are you feeling today?" And, Eara would respond with, "Oh Grams, I am feeling fairly good. My condition is getting better. It is not as bad as it could be. In fact after dialysis, sometimes I go out in the evening, dance and enjoy myself."

Fran's reply was, "Be careful, don't over do it, snookums. God bless you. God loves you and we love you."

"I love you too Grams and grampa Jess. Bye."

With this type of exemplary faith set before her, Eara now knew and understood that WHEN LOVE BELIEVES AND PROVIDES, that she "can do all things through Christ who strengthens her."

After finishing her time at the boarding school, Eara was able to take a GED test, which she passed, thereby earning a certificate of graduation from High School. She then enrolled in a couple of classes in preparation for Junior College. Having come through a season of sickness with kidney failure and then being able to make academic achievements (the latter which appeared hopeless in her earlier years), this was now a season of good times for Eara.

Yet, as the pendulum of life's circumstances swings us through seasons of good times, recovery from sadness, sickness and sorrow, it also swings us back into seasons of melancholy and unhappiness. Once and again, for Eara, as it is for many of us, this season of unhappiness was upon her. Eara became more and more unhappy because Andrea was controlling the Medicaid check being sent to her each month for her expenses. Knowing that Eara was unable to get a job at the present time due to not being fully recovered from her illness, who gave Andrea the right to control Eara's check, by giving Eara very little spending change? Sometimes those little gods, who think they are in charge of our lives, can make our lives a living hell.

As this too shall pass, Eara was able to move on. Momentarily, on the brighter side of life, one of Eara's cousins was graduating in 1991, from a law school in Washington, D.C. Andrea promised that Eara could attend the graduation ceremony. And, as always quick to respond and provide for Eara's needs, since she had few clothes, Fran sent Eara money for her to buy some new clothes for the trip. On his occasion, Todd even sent money for Eara's train fare. But, Andrea, for whatever reason "borrowed" the money and never re-paid Eara. So Eara did not get to go to the graduation ceremony. This was, of course, only one of many disappointments with which Eara had to contend. So, Fran discontinued sending so much money for Eara, knowing that Andrea would take it. And, once again, for Eara the brighter side of life became dim with melancholy.

To add insult to injury, about June or July of 1991, Andrea took a trip to Houston, Texas (probably financed by some, if not all of Eara's money she had been controlling), leaving Eara and the two smaller children at home in Troy, New York. While Andrea was off on a "wild goose chase" trip, for three weeks, in Texas, leaving Eara with the children and hardly any money to take care of the children and/or herself, a blood clot had developed in the fistula, which Eara had in her left arm. Complicating matters, Eara had to take dialysis by means of a catheter through her neck. This catheter had to be irrigated every day. Had Andrea returned to her old irresponsible, neglectful, self-centered self? What type of caring, loving and self-sacrificing mother would do such a thing to a sick daughter and her other two little children?

The situation had gotten so desperate for Eara, that she called Fran on a Saturday during Andrea's absence.

"Hi, Grams. Mother is still in Texas. We have no money for food or anything else. All of the food we got from the Food Pantry is gone. And, I am still sick as a dog. I can hardly make it. Plus, we have no transportation and I have to walk back and forth to the hospital when I need treatment. Thank God the hospital is close by! Can you help us?"

Desperate times call for desperate measures. So, Fran quickly gave an unequivocal response, "Of course I can and will help you." She hung up the phone and dashed out immediately to Western Union and sent money to them in order for them to eat.

After the three weeks, Andrea finally returned home with Jethro. He was now eighty-six years old. Andrea gave Jethro Eara's bedroom to sleep in. In turn, Eara now had to bunk on the living room couch for sleeping purposes.

This entire scenario made Fran very angry and of course she lit into Andrea.

"You have not changed. You are still as irresponsible, negligent and self-centered as you have always been. I thought by now, you would have matured into a more caring, faithful, humble, loving, patient, peaceful, providing, sacrificing, self-controlled mother! But you ain't changed one bit!"

"And you ain't changed either. You need to step off. Do you hear me?" Blip.

Fran later learned in talking with Eara that Andrea often nagged her so much about receiving Fran's wrath, that she (Eara) was encouraged to become liberated and emancipated.

So we have seen through Fran's steadfast love for her granddaughter that WHEN LOVE BELIEVES AND PROVIDES LOVE can bestow courage and strength to overcome seasons of:

- Seemingly discontentment and melancholy,
- Broke-ness and brokenness,
- Alleged promiscuous behavior,
- Living in a chaotic and demeaning mess,
- Continued disappointment, lying, negligence, and irresponsibility,
- Academic failure,
- Youthful exuberance,
- Severe sickness,
- Living in the valley of dry bones.

Six
When Love Abides

WHEN LOVES ABIDES, LOVE gives all it possesses to the downtrodden. LOVE is patient and is kind. LOVE does not envy, does not boast, is not proud, is not rude, is not self-seeking, does not delight in evil and is not easily angered. LOVE keeps no record of wrongs but rejoices with the truth. WHEN LOVE ABIDES, LOVE, always protects, trusts, hopes, perseveres. WHEN LOVE ABIDES, LOVE instills faithfulness, gentleness, goodness, joy, kindness, love, patience peace and self-control. When LOVE fulfills these attributes, LOVE brings fragmented lives together. WHEN LOVE ABIDES, this LOVE is invisible. Many times one can't see this LOVE but one can feel its all encompassing power as it instills the courage and strength to move on to a higher level of expectancy.

Let us see how Fran and Jess smothered Eara with this kind of Abiding Love and what effect it had on Eara as she now moves through life's experiences from 18–24.

On October 17, 1991, Eara turned eighteen years old and by now, she said she had met a very nice boyfriend, by the name of Steven Haas. It seemed that he was very kind and attentive to her from the way she talked.

As the Thanksgiving and holiday seasons were fast approaching, Fran, although ever concerned about Eara's health, was desperate and longing to see her and to meet Eara's boyfriend to appraise him.

So, one evening Fran called Eara.

"Hi, baby girl. It's Grams. Can arrangements be made for your dialysis treatments, such that you could come and spend the holidays with grandpa Jess and me, if you would like to come?" Very excited Eara responded.

"O, yes Grams that would be lovely. I would also like to spend the holidays with Steve. Is it ok to invite Steve to come?" Thereupon, Fran enquired if Steve was there and asked that he be put on the phone.

"Hello, Steve. This is Eara's grandmother Fran. I wish to invite you to come with her to spend the holidays with us. Is that ok with you?"

"Yes, Mrs. Baldwin. I'll be there."

After they hung up the phones, Eara called her doctor to see if it was ok for her to travel by Greyhound Bus to Dayton. He gave his blessing and Eara called Grams back to report.

"Hi, Grams, it is me. The doctor said I could and I feel I am able to ride the bus. Steve would be with me, so hopefully, all will go well."

"Thanks for the good news, baby girl. We'll see the two of you when you get in town. Bye."

After they arrived and the grandparents met Steve all went well for a short period of time. Fran's appraisal was that Steve seemed to be a very nice person and he was quite attentive to Eara. Jess and Fran enjoyed their company; however, their visit was shortened due to Eara's blood clotting, preventing her from getting her third dialysis treatment, so Fran had to send them home by plane.

Follow-up conversations with Eara revealed Eara had more than health problems to deal with, as usual.

During one conversation when Fran had called, Eara told her, "Grams, I am very unhappy being in this rat-infested house and neighborhood. In addition, since mother is no longer in control of my money, she keeps on badgering me to get out. And, I cannot afford to do so right now."

"Don't worry, baby girl, as LOVE would have its way, your blessing is coming soon. Just hold out and hold on for a little while longer."

As soon as they hung up the phones, Fran called Todd.

In January of 1992, Todd visited with Eara and leased an apartment for her. He furnished the kitchen and bedroom. Fran furnished her living room, as well as all of her bed linen, curtains and accessories. Sometime later, Todd sent her a microwave oven and Fran sent lamps, etc.

As Eara's life and circumstances appeared to be coming together, after several months, she stated that she was planning to have a roommate move in to help bear the expenses. However, as it turned out, Steve was the roommate. Naturally, Fran was disappointed in learning about the person who became the roommate and she did not hesitate to express her disapproval. After weighing all of the circumstances surrounding Eara's current life style, Fran's disapproval meant little.

In moving on down life's highway, sometime in June of 1992, Fran called Eara and was unable to get an answer. After several calls, she decided to call Andrea's number. One of the children answered and informed Fran that Eara had received a kidney and was in the hospital.

"I am elated, but I am resentful of the fact that you guys did not think to call me with such important news."

"Madame, I am sorry, we did not call. But mother did not want you to worry. Knowing how you are."

After two days, the transplant failed. Later, it was decided that Eara would have peritoneal dialysis. Immediately after the catheter was implanted, Eara developed an infection, became very ill and was in the hospital for more than a week. The catheter was necessarily removed. After a few months a new fistula was put into her arm. It seemed to work successfully for a while.

By now it was August of 1992 and Fran and Jess once again drove to New York to visit with Eara for a few days. While she was home, Eara appeared to be happy in her little apartment and was in good spirits. Moreover, Eara and Steve were very happy and apparently he was so very kind to her. As a matter of fact, as Eara told the story, she can call upon him at any time and in every case, no matter what, when, where, how or why she had to go to the emergency ward at the hospital, sometimes in the middle of the night, Steve would come and walk with her or, if necessary he would call an ambulance for her. What a man. All women wish for one like him. Again, realizing that all appeared well, Fran and Jess returned to Dayton. And, once again by their presence, Eara knew that she would be well for a while because ABIDING LOVE was near.

During the next year, Eara and Steve became closer and began to talk of marriage. However, Steve was unable to find work at the time and Eara felt it was useless to marry under those circumstances.

Realizing that Eara now was not only dealing with intermittent bouts of kidney failures but also she was dealing with rising health and living costs, Fran as usual attempted to alleviate some of Eara's problems by asking and inviting her again to move to Ohio, in order to be closer to her family. However, Fran's indwelling spirit of ABIDING LOVE, gave Eara the courage to decline Fran's offer and she didn't want to leave New York.

By the fall of 1993, Eara began to experience more trouble. The fistula became infected again. The doctor again suggested peritoneal dialysis. Eara called Fran and said that she was really paranoid just thinking about such surgery. However, a vein was taken from her leg and placed in her arm, but that surgery wasn't successful. Eara spent two months in the hospital at that time and became very depressed. It seemed that nothing, which was done, was working. Finally, it was decided that peritoneal dialysis was the only answer at the time. Fran encouraged Eara to try to adjust to it and pray that everything would be all right. During Eara's stay in the hospital, Fran called several times a week. She sent flowers and did everything to encourage her and make her happy. Most of all, Fran wanted to let Eara know, that:

- She was loved and never neglected by her grandparents.
- She was very brave young lady.
- Though she never asked for help and knowing that her sustenance was very meager, her grandmother was always there to send her a small check to buy something for herself, for which she was grateful.

Several months had now passed since Eara's last bout in the hospital. At first Eara complained about the peritoneal dialysis, but Fran encouraged her to try and adjust to it because at the time it seemed to be best for her. Nonetheless, apparently, at this point in time she was doing well as she reported to Fran.

"Grams, I feel well. I've taken a bus tour to an amusement park in New Jersey and I spent the day without any ill effects. I am also working a few hours a week at a fast-food chain. In addition, I am working out at the Y several times a week."

Fran was again elated to hear this report, but added: "Baby girl, this news sounds wonderful. And, I am glad you are enjoying something other than staying home and watching television. But, be careful. Don't do too much at the same time. Love you, always. Bye."

As Eara's health condition was steadily and progressively improving, so were her family and other relationships. Todd visited her more often and their relationship improved greatly. Out of this context, Todd also visited (via Eara's suggestion perhaps) with his mother and dad for several weeks and from all indications was doing well. As for Andrea, she and Eara developed a more amicable relationship and occasionally visited each other. Out of this more amicable relationship, apparently Eara did not mind taking care of one of the younger children left there during the fall when Andrea went to Texas, again. In fact, Eara loved her little sisters very much and was glad to be near them.

By this time, Steve and Eara became "an item" and for four years seemed very much in love. He continued to be the kind, sweet Steve whom Fran and Jess first met. Eara needed someone who loved her and was loyal.

In Fran's estimation, she was sure that, that is what Eara found in Steve. As Fran watched Steve act she too came to the realization this is the one for Eara. In fact, in Fran's appraisal of Steve, she felt, one could not help but to admire and appreciate Steve for his kindness toward

Eara. He stood by when her dad and mother could not be there. Fran finally came to realize that Eara had her life to live and her happiness was what mattered. Eara seemed happy, and if with Steve, then so be it.

Fran also came to realize Eara loved to be loved, and who doesn't? Yet, this is why Fran contacted her regularly—to reassure her of the love her grandparents have for her (not so much as a replacement of Steve's love).

From this point, Fran would ruminate about she and Eara's relationship overtime. On many summer days, she could be found sitting on her porch, smiling as she watched the neighborhood children alight from the school bus as she did every day while Eara was in school. Out of these visions, Fran often became teary-eyed because she became haunted by the fact that perhaps, had she not given up custody, she could have spared Eara some of the poverty, hunger, negligence, stress and sickness which she endured.

But beyond the tears, what Fran was really experiencing was the boomerang effect of ABIDING LOVE. This is the type of love that as it is given out, in time so does this love come back to the distributor of such love.

This love came back to its source in August 1995. During this month, Eara had visited with Fran and Jess and they spent a wonderful two weeks together. Fran noticed Eara's health appeared to be fairly good. She and Fran attended church during one of the weekends and it made Fran happy to see that Eara was able to find and read the Scripture for the service. This was also a surprise for Fran, since she doubted that Eara attended church at all, given her lifestyle and circumstances in New York. Those members of the church who knew her were happy to see her, and she was happy to be welcomed by them. After the service, Eara and Grams went out to dinner and talked a great deal of "times past."

During this visit, Eara and Fran also had time to go shopping together. Eara wanted to go to the flea market, but time would not permit. They went out and had dinner, again, and consequently Eara had only a very short time to spend with her friend, Yolanda. Jess was out of town that weekend and the two of them spent endless hours together talking, laughing, playing Rummy and having fun. On the morning Eara was to leave, one of Fran's friends came to say goodbye.

Fran's heart was heavy as always when Eara was leaving. Strangely, it was no different than in years previous when she would leave. It was obvious that Eara was a bit sad at leaving and when Fran's friend asked if she wanted to leave, Eara replied, "Oh, no. I could stay with Grams forever and be happy."

At this point, Fran began to hope that perhaps her prayers might be answered and that Eara may decide to return home, to Ohio. This has been Fran's prayer for many years. Was it finally going to happen?

After a wonderful two weeks, Eara went home and she and Fran regularly talked via the phone. However, when Fran tried to pump Eara for information about her mother, Eara became evasive and divulged very little information. At one time when Fran said to her, "You look so much like your mother." Eara responded with some hostility.

"Please, don't ever say that again."

Apparently, all was not well between Eara and her mother. Yet, with ABIDING LOVE AND GRACE for her mother's sake, Eara kept her younger sisters, who spent quite a bit of time at her apartment. In fact, she told Fran that many times the youngsters stayed all night because they also hated to go home.

While Fran and Eara's relationship was continuing to cement a firm bond between the two, at this point in the ongoing saga of Eara's life, one wonders what additional impact did Todd, Andrea and Steve bring into her life.

Well, Todd finally retired and came home to live in Ohio. His attitude seemed to have changed and he acted more like his old self. Hopefully he was happy. It was evident, however, that Todd had a great deal of influence over Eara, and it appeared that he wanted to be in complete control. One can only hope Todd's desire would not cause a resurgence of animosity between he and Fran. This would be a harrowing experience for Eara to live through again.

In staying with Andrea's case, it has become obvious Andrea was becoming more and more a drug-addicted, neglectful and irresponsible mother just as she was in the early days of Eara's life. It is no wonder Eara hated when Fran would compare her to Andrea. Now that Eara has become older and wiser and having experienced life's pitfalls, perhaps she now disdains what her mother haphazardly is attempting to re-introduce into her life and that of her younger sisters.

Unlike her mother, Steve perhaps was not introducing drug addictions into her life, but by Eara's admission to Fran, she and Steve were not quite so close as they used to be. Whatever baggage he was trying to impact her life with, Eara was now older and wiser and perhaps was ready to "lay aside the weight." She was ready to set aside Steve's baggage to the point that she intimated to Fran that she might like to return solo to Ohio to live.

The latter prospect, of course, would make Fran, Jess and Todd very happy.

The Thanksgiving and Christmas holidays of 1996 passed quickly that year and there was an air of inner peace and yet sadness in the family household.

It was the Saturday, three weeks before Christmas. Fran was busy planning for the day and Jess was putting up the decorations. Fran told him not to forget to hang Eara's stocking in the center mantle. This is the stocking which Eara had for Christmas 1981, the first year she came to make her home with her grandparents. Fran kept it and hung it each year. Through this stocking Fran and Jess were able to feel the presence of Eara's ABIDING LOVE. Like many other Christmases when she was not there, just feeling the spirit of her LOVE brought inner peace and joy to Fran's and Jess's hearts, minds and souls.

On the other hand, there was a feeling of sadness during this holiday season of 1996. Fran and Jess were aging. And, specifically Fran missed sending the huge box of goodies and gifts which she usually sent to Eara at Christmas time. Fran would have liked noting better than having Eara with the family for Christmas. However, with air transportation so expensive that year, Fran could not afford it, especially since she had paid for Eara's round-trip airline ticket just a few months ago.

But WHEN LOVE ABIDES, miraculous things do happen. For, suddenly the phone rang and upon answering Fran heard a familiar voice.

"Hello, Grams, I am making arrangements to move to Ohio!"

Fran was overcome with happiness. In tears she said, "Great! When are you coming? Oh, this makes me so happy."

"There is some important business I have to attend to, due to my condition, but I hope to be home by the early part of next year. I love you, Grams. Bye."

After hanging up the phones, Fran pondered on the fact that Eara finally decided to come home and she thought, it seemed like a long time to wait, but FOR THE LOVE OF A GRAND one could wait forever.

During the summer of 1997, Eara came to Dayton, but she didn't come "home!" Why?

For several months, Todd had been living in an apartment building, very near where his parents lived. Since there was a vacant apartment upstairs over his, he furnished one room (the bedroom) and moved Eara into it. What was Todd's reasoning or motive behind such a move? Surely he was not trying to regurgitate old animosities, was he?

Secretly knowing that Eara's income was very limited, Fran hoped that Eara would stay with her grandparents until she would be able to secure her own apartment. Fran also thought that such an opportunity would have given Eara a chance to save her income and to accumulate a little before paying rent. This thought occurred to Fran particularly since Eara's rent in New York was only a few dollars a month and the rent in Dayton was much more than a few dollars. In any event Fran did not want to discourage her.

Furthermore when in conversation with Todd he told Fran, "Eara would never do that."

Todd was obviously letting Fran know that he was in control of Eara's welfare and that she might as well forget her desires and wishes of having Eara to live with grandparents. In this regard Fran was wise enough not to pursue the issue any further.

However, since the only the bedroom in Eara's apartment was furnished, Fran took her to a store and purchased a small dinette set and a two-piece living room set for the apartment. Eara seemed very pleased at the time.

Though Todd may have basically taken care of Eara's temporal needs, it was Fran and Jess who provided more of Eara's human bonding and spiritual needs. For the first few weeks, Eara visited with Fran and Jess often. Jess and Eara, together, planted the beautiful gardenias in the grandparents' backyard. When it came to mealtime, Eara often ate meals with her grandparents. Fran even bought her a couple of new dresses. This also brought joy and happiness to Eara's face and heart. Further, Fran bonded closer with Eara by taking her to act as a hostess for a formal dance, which Jess' Shriner's Club was hosting. Fran thought such an opportunity might give Eara a chance to see and meet "society" in action, as well as for her to meet some of her grandparents' friends. During the entire phase of new orientation, Eara seemed to enjoy herself.

A few months later, Todd moved to another apartment and even though he wanted to take Eara with him, Eara preferred staying where she was. And, while she remained there, Todd kept on searching for an apartment for her. An apartment which he thought Eara could financially manage. As fate would have it, Eara finally found an apartment, centrally located and convenient to most of the places where she would be going.

During the few ensuing months, Fran noticed that Eara's visits became much less frequent. Days and even weeks sometimes passed when Fran didn't hear from nor saw Eara. Naturally, this bothered Fran somewhat because she had hoped that she and Eara would still have the close, loving relationship that they had when Eara was living with her grandparents.

Nevertheless, Fran (being the Christian person she has always attempted to exemplify in her acts of ABIDING LOVE) never mentioned the pain of Eara's choice of separation between the two. Being "the bigger person," Fran never said a mumbling word about her feelings to Eara or to Todd. In fact, Fran always made it a point to hide her true unhappy feelings. Were her actions passiveness or sacrificing?

At this point in Eara's life she is now twenty-four years old and is working part-time and attending Junior College. In spite of her illness, her condition is stabilized and she appears to be happy. Most of all, Fran is happy to have her near and is proud of her and feels that her prayers have not been in vain. Why?

Well, it might be because WHEN LOVE ABIDES, there is no need for constant reminders. Eara daily knew and felt this indwelling LOVE. This is the kind of LOVE that:

- Roses cannot express,
- No amount of money can pay for,
- Material things cannot replace,
- Lays down its life for another,
- Bears all, endures all, conquers all,
- Interacts with hope,
- Believes all things,
- Provides all things, at no charge,
- Lingers 24 x 7 x 365,
- Abides forever.

As a matter of fact, not long ago, Fran called to give Eara a message. After a brief conversation, Eara hesitated and said, "Is that all you have to say?"

Fran asked if there were anything else and Eara then said, "Grams, I miss you and want to see you. I love you, Grams."

Fran then replied, "I love you too, baby girl." Fran then smiled, turned her eyes toward heaven and said, "Thank you, God, FOR THE LOVE OF A GRAND."